Hell Squad: Niko

Anna Hackett

Niko

Published by Anna Hackett
Copyright 2016 by Anna Hackett
Cover by Melody Simmons of eBookindiecovers
Edits by Tanya Saari

ISBN (eBook): 978-0-9945572-9-2
ISBN (paperback): 978-1-925539-07-3

What readers are saying about Anna's Science Fiction Romance

At Star's End – One of Library Journal's Best E-Original Romances for 2014

Return to Dark Earth – One of Library Journal's Best E-Original Books for 2015 and two-time SFR Galaxy Awards winner

The Phoenix Adventures – SFR Galaxy Award Winner for Most Fun New Series and "Why Isn't This a Movie?" Series

Beneath a Trojan Moon – SFR Galaxy Award Winner and RWAus Ella Award Winner

Hell Squad – Amazon Bestselling Science Fiction Romance Series and SFR Galaxy Award for best Post-Apocalypse for Readers who don't like Post-Apocalypse

The Anomaly Series – #1 Amazon Action Adventure Romance Bestseller

Chapter One

Though some might protest about being on base patrol, she didn't mind it. Mackenna Carides lifted her carbine and stepped carefully through the long grass, her gaze scanning ahead for anything out of the ordinary.

She had to admit, though, she still wasn't used to the lack of trees around their new home. This place was nothing like Blue Mountain Base.

It'd been over a year and a half since aliens had invaded Earth. A year and a half since the dinosaur-like raptors had sent down their ships and troops and decimated the planet. Mac, and her fellow soldiers in the Army of the Coalition of United Countries, had been part of the military response. Her jaw hardened. She'd watched a lot of friends die in the fighting. She'd fought for days on end, pulled survivors out of raptor claws, and finally found a haven in a secret underground military base in the Blue Mountains west of Sydney.

But now, even that was gone.

Mac ducked through a large gap in a sagging fence. Several weeks ago, the aliens had finally sniffed them out and attacked Blue Mountain Base. In a wild and dangerous move, the human survivors had formed a convoy and made a mad dash out of the mountains.

It had ended here. At a new haven built in an old underground coal mine. The Enclave.

"Man, I am enjoying the food here."

Mac turned to look at her patrol partner. Camryn McNabb was tall, slim, and gorgeous. Everyone on their squad called her the glamazon. With short, dark hair, dark skin inherited from her African mother, and that long, lean body, Cam knew exactly how to work what she'd been born with. Right now, though, she was covered with black carbon fiber armor, and she carried her carbine in an easy, familiar grip.

"We had good food at Blue Mountain," Mac said.

"Never said we didn't," Cam continued. "But that garden they have here...they grow all sorts of great stuff. Have you seen the raspberries?"

"Yeah." Mac had stolen a few—big, juicy, and damned delicious. She would never admit it to a soul, but she had a secret addiction to decadent tastes and smells. She hid her vice under her tough reputation. At barely an inch over five feet, her fellow soldiers tended to underestimate her. She made sure they only ever did it once.

She looked over at Cam. In Mac's entire military career, she'd never been a part of a team as good as this one. All the squads were made up of survivors from every branch of the military and law enforcement. Squad Nine's leader was Roth

Masters—a tough, no-nonsense soldier. Mac considered him a hell of a boss and a friend. Apart from Roth and the big, silent Theron, the rest of the squad was all women. They respected the hell out of each other, had saved each other's backs too many times to count. They worked side-by-side with the other squads, including the infamous Hell Squad, and every day, they did their bit to protect their group of human survivors and fight back against the aliens.

She scanned the landscape—rolling hills covered with green grass and stands of trees. The Enclave had been built by the former President of the United Coalition. Instead of fighting for his people, he'd made a deal with the Gizzida aliens, and built this small, cozy Enclave. He'd then selected a small group of people he'd determined deserved to be saved.

Bastard. President Howell was dead now, and Mac couldn't bring herself to feel very sorry about it. Now, the Enclave was filled to the brim with its original survivors, and with those who'd escaped the onslaught of the Blue Mountain Base attack. It had only been two weeks, and they were all still finding a way to live together. She figured it was going to take longer until they all trusted each other. Still, Cam was right—the food was damn good.

Mac's earpiece crackled to life. "Mac? Cam? You two there?"

It was the smooth, calm voice of Arden, their squad's comms officer. She was beneath their feet

3

inside the Enclave, in the secure comms control room.

"Receiving," Mac answered.

"I have Lia from the drone team on the line. She wants to talk to you. Seems that she's having some issues with one of her drones."

Mac touched her ear. "Put her through."

A second later another voice came on the line. "Hi, Mackenna. This is Lia."

"What can we do for you, Lia?"

"We have a drone out to the south of the Enclave on standard reconnaissance. It seems to be jammed, and its feed isn't getting back to us. None of the other drones are picking up any alien activity. Can you check it out and see what's going on?"

Mac scanned the sky to the south. She didn't see anything there, but the drones—tiny quadcopters that could fit in the palm of her hand—were hard to spot. Plus, they all had small illusion systems that rendered them near-invisible to alien sensors, and blurred them on visual. The only thing Mac could see in the blue sky was a bird soaring high overhead.

"No problem. We'll head that way and take a look."

"Thanks," Lia answered. "Let me know if you find anything. I'm guessing it's just a malfunction, but I want to make sure."

Mac nodded her head toward the south. "We need to go and check on a drone."

The two of them headed that way, picking their

way through the long grass. All around the Enclave, the landscape appeared undisturbed and overgrown. The security team worked hard to ensure there were no tracks or obvious signs of occupation. Mac knew the place also had state-of-the-art defenses, and they could completely lock down in the event of an attack.

But the key thing helping to keep them safe was the small fleet of drones. They were vitally important for providing intel for the squads. When the aliens had first attacked, they'd destroyed all the planet's satellite systems. Luckily, Noah Kim, the tech genius at Blue Mountain Base, had repurposed drones so that an expert team could fly them and provide information on the aliens' whereabouts. That information was fed to all the squads and without it, they were blind.

It was a brilliant, sunny day, and, for a second, Mac could almost imagine that the invasion had never happened. Right here, at this spot, all she saw were beautiful hills, blue sky, and bright sunshine. Birds were chirping, and from here there was no sign of the destruction the aliens had wreaked. She knew just to the north lay the remains of Sydney, the former capital of the Coalition. Nothing was left of the once-thriving city, other than rubble and dust.

Mac released a long breath. Damn, she was still feeling a little raw and twitchy after their wild race out of the mountains. The aliens had come close to capturing them numerous times. People had died. She closed her eyes for a second. It still hadn't fully sunk in that they were somewhere safe.

"I do miss the old base," Cam said, "but man, I *love* the swimming pool."

Mac smiled. The Enclave's indoor, heated swimming pool was proving very popular. Personally, Mac liked the Garden. It was accessed through a long tunnel, and sat up on top of an escarpment. It was built inside a bowl of rock and open to the sky—but with a retractable roof, in case of danger. It got lots of natural sunlight. Something she'd missed in the rabbit warren of Blue Mountain Base. And she was pretty darn happy with the fancy, well-equipped gym here, as well.

But, as she spotted an abandoned processing plant from the old mine, the metal rusting and sagging, her hands clenched on her carbine. She knew she couldn't fully relax, couldn't let the luxurious surrounds of the Enclave let her go soft. They were at war, in a fight for their very existence. She needed to be in peak physical condition and ready for anything.

It was one of the things her father had taught her. *No tears, little girl. Toughen up and face that problem head-on.* She thought of her father and her two brothers. As far as she knew, they were dead. Her brothers had been somewhere in Texas when the first wave of the invasion had hit. Her father had been on an oil rig off the north of Scotland. Her chest went tight. She'd never heard from them, and the one message she'd ever gotten through to one of the survivor outposts in Texas hadn't received a response.

Mac's mother had died when she was young and her father had dragged Mac and her brothers around the world as he'd worked on different oil rigs. There had been no chance to collect precious things, or get used to a certain house or place. She'd learned never to depend on anything, because it could be gone in a blink.

"I don't see any drones," Cam said. "No aliens, either."

Mac didn't see anything out of the norm, either. She looked around again, and once again watched the beautiful bird—some sort of hawk or eagle—dipping and flowing overhead. She touched her ear. "Lia? No sign of your drone, and no sign of any alien activity that might be jamming it."

"Thanks, Mac. The intermittent signal is coming from about ten meters west of your current location."

"On it." Mac wandered toward a lone tree in that direction.

Then she spotted the drone snagged in the branches.

"Looks like some drone pilot is going to get a ribbing from their colleagues," Cam murmured with a smile.

Mac smiled and touched her earpiece. "Lia, we found it. Hung up in a tree."

Lia's expulsion of breath came across the line. "Damn. Must be a malfunction. I'll talk to Noah and his tech team, and see if we can work out what happened to it."

"Roger that. We'll bring it back in for you." Mac

looked at Cam. "Ready to go climbing?"

Cam scowled. "Why me?"

"Because I outrank you."

"You never pull rank."

"I do when it comes to looking like an idiot climbing a tree."

Muttering under her breath, Cam climbed the wide trunk of the tree and pulled herself up into the branches. After a few minutes and a few more curses, she'd freed the little drone.

As Cam dropped it down, Mac caught it and watched as Cam dropped down as well, landing in a light crouch. Mac turned the drone over.

"Hell, it's pretty battered." One of the rotors was mangled, and the side of it was dented.

"Yep, someone is going to catch hell for crashing this little baby," Cam said.

A second later, Arden was back on the comm line. "Mac, there's a war meeting in the Command Center. All squad leaders and their second-in-commands have been requested to attend. Roth said he'll meet you there. A relief team will come out shortly to take over patrol from you guys."

War meeting. *Great.* "On my way."

Cam and Mac headed back toward the entrance they'd used to exit the Enclave. It was cleverly hidden in the ground, and impossible to find if you didn't know where it was. As they approached, she saw two other soldiers leaving the Enclave to take over patrol.

Mac couldn't help but grin. These two were from Hell Squad—the toughest, meanest, most efficient squad around. It was headed by the battle-hardened Marcus Steele, but the two coming toward her were Hell Squad's sole female soldier and its sniper. The two also happened to be crazy in love, and had just recently finally admitted it to each other.

Shaw Baird was tall, slightly lanky, with shaggy hair streaked with gold. When he spotted Mac and Cam, he shot them a flirtatious grin. Mac was pretty sure flirting was in the man's DNA. In addition to being an excellent shot with his long-range laser rifle, he'd also been a notorious ladies' man before he'd finally faced his feelings for Claudia Frost.

Beside him, Claudia stood tall and straight, her dark hair pulled back in a long braid. There was no doubting from the badass look on her face that she could quite easily take down a raptor twice her size. Mac had seen her in action, and would have the former SAS soldier on her team any day.

Mac watched as Shaw leaned in to Claudia and whispered something. The woman rolled her eyes and gave the man a smack in the arm. That just made him grin more wildly.

A relationship like this, love…it had to soften a woman. Claudia didn't look any different—except for the light in her eyes when she looked at her lover—but surely that love would eventually seep in, and make that tough look on her face disappear. Mac knew that had to be a weakness.

"Nothing much to report," Mac said. "I suspect you guys will just have a lovely stroll in the sun."

"After the last few months," Shaw said, "a stroll in the sun sounds damn nice."

"We just rescued a drone for Lia." Mac held up the small quadcopter. "Landed in a tree."

"Malfunction?" Claudia asked.

Mac shrugged. "Looks that way. The geek squad is going to take a look at it. Certainly no aliens around."

"You two stay alert." Cam's grin was a little cheeky. "No hanky-panky."

Shaw waggled his eyebrows. "But I'm so good at hanky-panky."

That earned him a whack on the back of the head from Claudia.

They waved goodbye, and Mac and Cam climbed down through the hatch and dropped into the tunnel.

"I'll drop you at the Command Center and then take the drone to the tech lab," Cam said. "After that, I'm off to the pool." She rubbed her hands together with glee.

Mac handed over the drone as they headed out of the tunnel and into a wide, carpeted corridor. Ahead, people were walking in small groups, talking and laughing.

This was where the true differences to Blue Mountain Base were really noticeable. There was thick, plush carpet on the floor, and framed artwork lining the corridor walls. It didn't quite mask the fact that they were underground, but it had a state-of-the-art lighting system that mimicked natural light. Blue Mountain Base had felt like a concrete rabbit warren of military tunnels, and while they'd all done their best to make it seem like a home, it hadn't ever come close to the Enclave's luxurious feel.

They made their way through the corridors— Mac was finally learning her way around. They reached the Command Center, and passed the large glass windows that looked into the high-tech hive of activity. There were walls covered in flat screens, and multiple comp stations set up with various people working at them. In the main meeting area in the center, she saw most of the squad leaders and their seconds were already there.

Then she spotted *him*.

Nikolai Ivanov was one of the leaders of the Enclave. He stood in front of the group in jeans and a dark T-shirt. In the two weeks she'd been here, she'd done her best to avoid him. Something about the man made her itch. He was an artist, but she'd seen him in the field once when they'd first reached the Enclave. He might paint, but he was no simple artist.

After their convoy had arrived, Roth had been assigned to Niko to trade information and bring him up to speed on all the squads' capabilities. Roth had delegated the job to Mac.

So she'd been forced to spend a few tense hours meeting with Niko in his office. The man had this way of watching her... She brushed the thought away. She was probably just being silly. The man was an artist and clearly liked to watch people.

She looked at him now through the glass. A long, lean body, dark hair that was close to brushing his shoulders. Although she couldn't see them from this distance, she knew his eyes were a piercing green.

Then he looked up, and his gaze hit hers unerringly.

Mac held it, not letting herself fall for the panicked need to look away. She felt the punch of heat to her belly, absorbed it with annoyance.

Then she broke contact and looked away. If she ignored this *thing*, it would go away.

"What was that?"

Cam's voice made Mac jolt. "What?"

"Oh, don't play coy with me, Carides. What the hell was that look I just saw? That panty-melting, I-want-to-lick-you-all-over look that the man—that handsome, sexy-as-sin, artist man—just gave you."

Mac resisted the urge to stiffen. It would just give Cam more fuel. "I didn't see anything."

"Mac, you see everything. Girl, the man is *hot*. And if you missed it, I said hot with underlined, italicized letters."

Mac sniffed. "Aren't you going swimming?"

Cam's dark gaze narrowed. "You toss every man over your shoulder and slam him into the training mats. Why not have a little fun for a change? Drag this one down and ride him like a pony."

"Cam!" Mac hated that she could picture that image of her and Niko far too clearly.

"What are two lovely ladies like you doing in a place like this?"

Cam stiffened like she'd been hit with an electric prod, and Mac barely suppressed a smile. *Saved by the berserkers.*

The two men striding down the corridor were the leader and second of Squad Three, better known as the berserkers. These men were wild. The berserkers had been cobbled together from men with...dubious backgrounds. Mercenaries, bikers, and...well, it was best not to ask too many questions.

Tane and Hemi were brothers, although Tane was a little taller and leaner than his brother, with a harsh, handsome face that was framed by heavy dreadlocks. He stalked closer with a stride that reminded Mac of a big jungle cat. Hemi was rougher, stockier, and had a dark beard that didn't hide his wide smile. He sauntered like a rock star and his gaze was firmly on Cam.

"Rahia, just keep your mouth shut," Cam bit out. "Every time you open it, you make me want to punch you." Her smile took on an edge. "And I'm still in my armor, so that means I can really hurt you."

"Aw, Camryn, you still angry with me about that whole pink helmet incident? Isn't it time to forgive me?"

Mac winced. "Hemi, it's best you don't bring up the 'painting the helmet pink' thing."

"Why not?" Something wicked danced in his eyes. "Cam looks so pretty in pink."

Cam made a growling sound. She took a step forward, and then slammed her fist into Hemi's stomach. To the man's credit, he barely doubled over, but the air did rush out of him. Cam had a hell of a right hook.

"Tane." Cam nodded at Squad Three's leader.

Tane gave her a nod and a faint smile, then Cam sauntered down the corridor like a model on a catwalk.

Mac looked at Hemi. "Dude, I don't know what your game is, but I really don't think pissing Cam off all the time is a good way to sweet-talk her into your bed."

Hemi grinned. "She'll come around. I have a certain charm."

Mac shook her head and pushed open the doors to the Command Center, the men moving to follow her.

She headed to where Roth was standing with Marcus Steele and Hell Squad's second in command, Cruz Ramos and his partner, Santha Kade. Mac nodded at some of the other squad leaders, but avoided looking toward the front of the room.

It didn't matter, dammit. She was still very conscious that Niko's gaze was on her the entire time. She could feel it like a physical touch.

She heaved out a breath. *Just ignore it. It'll go away.*

Chapter Two

Nikolai Ivanov shoved his hands into his pockets and listened to the squad leaders talking around him. At the last second, he realized he still had paint on his hands, and he'd just smeared it on his jeans. He mentally shrugged. Wasn't the first time, and he was sure it wouldn't be the last.

He was listening as Noah Kim, the brilliant tech genius who'd come from Blue Mountain Base, was talking about upgrading some of the systems at the Enclave. Niko had thought his tech team was good, but Kim had a magic touch with electronics. In the two weeks since he'd arrived, he'd already made the energy and lighting systems thirty percent more efficient. He was looking into the security systems next, and also talking about upgrading some wiring.

It would benefit everyone here.

Not everyone had agreed when Niko had invited the Blue Mountain Base survivors to join the Enclave. Before, everyone in the Enclave had been very comfortable, had found a sense of solace and safety in the horror of the alien invasion. Now, their haven was bursting at the seams. But it had been the right thing to do, and Niko didn't regret it for a second.

In this new world, humans had to stick together. Under Howell, it hadn't happened. Niko still burned with anger when he thought about how he'd fallen for the former president's lies. Howell had spun a compelling story—never once letting on that they'd all been handpicked for his secret little haven at the expense of the rest of the damn world.

Niko let out a breath. That was the past. The future was integrating the new survivors with the Enclave members. Making everyone into one cohesive group, making it a home for everybody.

He tuned back into the discussions as they turned to the security and military aspects. Niko stepped forward. "I've had extensive discussions with General Holmes this week. We've carefully weighed all the options and decided that it is best that General Holmes takes over security and military operations for the Enclave."

He saw the Blue Mountain Base squad leaders all nod. They respected the tall, dedicated man who had saved their lives and gotten them this far. Niko glanced over at Adam Holmes. He looked like a general—tall, with a straight bearing, and a distinguished dash of gray at his temples. He'd arrived here looking exhausted, tense, and stressed, but slowly, over the last two weeks, Niko had seen the man start to relax a little. It certainly helped that he had a sexy, blonde bombshell of a girlfriend.

Then Niko's gaze fell on the Enclave's head of

security, Captain Kate Scott. She'd been in charge of security all this time, running the place jointly with him. In her early forties and career military, she'd only ever had the best interests of the residents at heart. She'd been the first to suggest the Blue Mountain survivors come here.

He'd already briefed her on this decision, and she'd agreed it made sense. Still, he knew this must feel like a demotion, and she now had Adam Holmes as a boss. But Kate and her team had been security only...they needed the military expertise of the squads. They'd been out there actively fighting the aliens, taking the offensive. If they were going to do more than just be trapped here in the Enclave for the rest of their lives, they needed to work together, be one unified group.

Then his gaze fell on Mackenna Carides.

Now, there was one person he'd like to be more unified with.

She was dwarfed by the broad-shouldered forms of Roth and Marcus standing beside her, making her look almost delicate by contrast.

But Niko knew she was as tough as the carbon fiber of her armor.

Her black hair was pulled back in a tight ponytail, accenting a face full of interesting angles. Large, dark eyes were framed by long lashes and she had skin the color of bronze. He couldn't remember being so intrigued by a woman in a very long time. Tough but beautiful. Smart and straightforward. There were no lies, no pretense, no shades of gray to Mackenna. In their meetings over the last couple of weeks, she'd answered all his questions in simple, clear terms. He liked watching her, trying to work out what made her tick, while in return, she watched him with a vaguely suspicious look.

He also wanted to see what was beneath that carbon fiber exterior of hers.

Holmes started talking. "My survivors need some more time to recover." His blue gaze met Niko's. "As you know, some are still recovering from their injuries at the hands of the aliens, plus plenty are still stressed from our escape."

Niko felt his jaw tighten. He'd seen some of the ugly scars. He knew some might never fully recover. But he'd do whatever the hell they needed to give them a chance.

"But," Holmes continued, "their recovery aside, we still need to discuss a long-term plan to rid the Earth of the Gizzida."

Kate leaned forward. "You really believe that's an' option? That we can fight them off? Isn't that just going to put us all at more risk?"

The general clasped his hands at the small of his back, his face grim. "We have to find a way, Captain Scott. I do not believe the aliens have any intention of leaving any humans alive, or at least not changed into raptors in their genesis labs. They will not stop until they completely hunt us down."

Niko's gut hardened. He'd seen the images of the genesis labs and the results of the aliens' cruel experimentation.

"We need to do it for our children," Cruz said,

from beside Marcus. He reached out and clasped Santha's hand. The woman had a small, rounded belly, and Cruz placed his other hand protectively on top of it. "Do you want them to grow up trapped here forever? Stuck underground like rats in a maze? This isn't living."

Nyet. No, it wasn't. Niko had known this day would come.

"If we stop fighting—" this time it was Mackenna who spoke "—we go soft. We give up."

Niko nodded. "I agree we need to formulate a long-term plan. In order to do that, two things are vitally important. First, we need to make better contact with the other human survivors hidden around the world. I know you've been in sporadic contact with some bases."

Holmes nodded. "Before the aliens wised up and blocked our longer-range communications. Communication with the other human bases has been spotty at best."

"We need to find a way around that," Niko said. "The second thing, the most important thing, is that intel will be vital. We have to have a very clear picture of the alien numbers, what they are doing, and what they have planned. Your drone fleet will be vital to that plan. Your intelligence officers, as well."

Santha moved, and another man joined her—her second-in-command, Devlin Gray. Together, the two of them ran the intel team. From what Niko had heard, both of them were very good at sneaking into alien territory, gathering information, and coming back without being discovered.

"My team has been working on a comprehensive intelligence plan," Santha said. "As you might have guessed, Dev has been taking over more of the day-to-day operations." She waved a rueful hand at her belly.

Devlin Gray nodded at his boss. "We won't sugarcoat this. We still have large gaps in our intelligence. Areas we can't get into, or information that just doesn't make sense to us yet. But we are working on it."

The Englishman wore dark slacks, and a white, button-down shirt. There was an elegant grace to him that Niko, as an artist, could admire.

"We're working now to map out all alien installations in the area," Dev added. "And any key locations, as well as their numbers and tactics. Lia and her team are helping to plug a lot of gaps."

Lia Murphy pushed her red hair back over her shoulder. "My team is doing what we can to help. As we train new pilots, we're adding some extra drones. I've had some interest from some Enclave members who have flying experience. We're testing our capabilities and taking the drones further afield, closer into the alien installations."

"You can't risk getting in too close," a male voice said.

Niko turned his head and looked at the blond man. It took a second for his name to click. Finn Erickson, head Hawk pilot. The confident way the man leaned against the wall hinted at his ability to pilot the Hawk quadcopters in and out of the combat zones.

Lia straightened. "My pilots are very good at what they do, and they are getting better every day. We need to keep testing and pushing our capabilities..."

Finn pushed away from the wall. "Pilots? You know—"

Lia waved a dismissive hand, interrupting him. "I've heard it before." Her tone was exasperated. "I know you believe pilots have to be strapped onto whatever they're flying. My guys are better than that. They can fly something without being anywhere near it."

Niko coughed to hide a smile. He got the feeling this was an old argument.

"The work you are all doing is top rate," he said. "Mackenna has spent some time over the last two weeks, bringing me up to speed. Let's keep gathering intelligence and we'll soon work out a plan to strike the aliens right where it will hurt them." He turned over his wrist and looked at his watch. "As you know, tonight we are holding a welcome dinner. The kitchen staff has been working on a grand feast in honor of the Blue Mountain survivors."

Holmes nodded. "My people are excited. They haven't had much chance to let loose and celebrate."

"I think it's important, both for your survivors, and for the Enclave members. We need to let everyone enjoy each other, and have a good time.

It's important we knock down the barriers and for them to become *our* people."

Holmes nodded.

"I could eat," a muscular, bearded man said from the other side of the room.

There were good-natured grumbles from the other squad members. "Hemi, you're always thinking with your stomach," Cruz called out.

"Or his dick," someone else added.

Niko smiled. He'd heard some wild stories about the berserkers. He was pretty certain he'd get a firsthand view of it before too long. "We'll see everyone up at the Garden for the dinner in a few hours." As they filed out, Niko shifted his gaze. "Mackenna?"

She'd already turned to leave, and her spine stiffened. She turned, and even though her face was blank, she looked like he'd just condemned her to Death Row.

"I was hoping you had a few minutes to go over some things with me. In my office." He waved to the adjoining door.

She shrugged a shoulder. "Fine."

He really shouldn't find that grouchy tone sexy, or her armor-covered body so appealing.

He followed her into his office.

***

Mac had never been one for stuffy, glossy offices, but she had to admit, she loved Niko's.

It was off the Command Center, with a large

wooden desk and a spiffy looking chair that could belong in a Hawk cockpit.

What she liked most was the large painting he'd hung behind his desk. It was a huge square canvas depicting a stormy day, with lightning cracking through the churning clouds. In the center was a dark-haired woman standing on the edge of a cliff, a yawning, black abyss below. She wore an elegant red dress, the wind whipping the skirt out behind her.

It was her face that was the best. You could feel the emotion pulsing off her—torment, agony, anguish.

Mac dropped into a guest chair and watched Niko stalk around his desk. Damn, the man could move. He swaggered. Not with cocky arrogance like Hemi, it was more the feel of a captain striding across the deck of his ship. No, not a captain—a pirate. That was better.

"I wanted to go over some of the squad training you laid out. I want to ensure you have the facilities you need, and also discuss having some of Kate...Captain Scott's team try out for places on the squads. Some of them have extensive military experience."

There was the slightest hint of a Russian accent in his voice. She could admit to herself that she liked it. "Your gym is better than what we had, so as long as we limit civilian access during squad training times, that will be fine. I can work up a roster with the other squad leaders. With respect to Captain Scott's team...I think it's best you discuss that with the general."

Niko didn't sit in his chair; instead, he moved closer, and perched on the edge of the desk. He was too close, and she could feel the heat of him. She could also smell paint. She'd always thought the scent of paint was unpleasant...but mixed with Niko's scent it wasn't.

She shifted in her chair. *Keep it together, Mac.*

"I'd like to know what you think, Mackenna."

"I've told you that everyone calls me Mac." The way he drew out her name, like he was tasting every syllable, was disconcerting.

"I know." He had a faint smile on his face. "I prefer Mackenna."

She shifted again and stared over his shoulder. "You can't break up any squads. They've been working together, fighting together, and trust each other. I'd test out the captain's people and make a short list of those who can fill spots if..."

Niko drew a breath. "If a squad loses anyone."

She nodded. No one liked to think about it, but it happened.

"I know a lot of them want the chance to fight," he said. "They've done an excellent job on Enclave security, but many of them want to fight the raptors."

She nodded again. "Is that it?"

He moved and his leg brushed against hers. She was still wearing her armor, so she couldn't really feel the touch...but it still somehow burned through her.

"If this integration between our two groups is

going to work, we all need to make an effort."

She frowned. "Okay."

"You aren't trying very hard."

She sat up straighter. "What do you mean?"

He shook his head, a faint smile appearing on his lips. "Mackenna, I've been trying to get to know you, to put you at ease, but you never let your guard down."

She blinked. "Get to know me?"

He moved now, crouching in front of her. If she wasn't trapped in a chair, she would have stepped backward.

"Yes. And I don't mean like a friend. I mean like I want to know how your lips taste, and what sounds you'd make if I was touching you."

Mac thought her heart might have stopped beating. "No." A low whisper.

"Yes."

"No." She shook her head. "I'm a soldier, you're a...leader." She waved at the fancy office.

He arched a brow. "I'm a man. You're a woman. And an intriguing, smart, and sexy one."

"No."

He tilted his head. "I never pegged you for a snob."

She shot to her feet. "I'm not a snob."

She suddenly realized she was standing, and he was crouched in front of her. It shouldn't have been sexy, it shouldn't have been anything, but him before her, his face level with her thighs and him looking up with that glint in his eyes, it made the blood in her veins run hot.

"Prove it," he said in a silky tone, his accent a little deeper.

She pulled in a breath. "Niko, I have to go out there and fight every day. I have to keep myself, my squad mates, and the people here alive. I can't afford any distractions. I don't want any distractions."

He stood now and towered over her. She stared at his chest and the way his black T-shirt clung to his lean muscles. The heat that radiated off him was unreal, and he smelled like the appealing combination of paint and some type of citrus cologne.

"You need things to remind you of why you fight." He lifted a hand and Mac forced herself to stay in place. He tucked an escaped strand of hair off her face.

"You don't even know me."

He smiled. "I've been watching you for two weeks. Talking to you whenever I can. Counting down the minutes to every one of these meetings we've had. I want to know more."

His words made a panicky fear run through her. It wasn't that she was afraid of him. She was afraid of what he could make her feel.

Mac was afraid that letting this thing between them free would make it run wild and hot...and she'd happily drown in it to the exclusion of everything else.

She stepped backward. "I have to go."

He held her gaze a little longer. "Very well, retreat if you need to."

She clenched her teeth. "This is not retreating. This is me declining to engage in a fruitless encounter."

Niko's hand shot out and gripped her arm. "Fruitless?" His tone was low and ruthless. "I'm going to prove you wrong, Mackenna. You can fortify those defenses of yours, but be warned, I'm very good at sneaking in behind enemy lines." He let her go, and now his voice morphed into a normal, friendly tone. "I'll see you at the dinner."

Mac turned, her heart beating rapidly as she left. Why did she feel like she'd just awakened a sleeping dragon? And she was the hungry beast's target.

Chapter Three

After a quick shower and a change of clothes, Niko made his way up to the Garden. As he entered the large area, he smiled at the people already gathered. A few called out hellos and waved. There was a mix of Enclave members and Blue Mountain Base survivors.

Lights were strung up in the trees, and overhead, the stars twinkled in the night sky. An illusion system made the Garden appear as just another patch of trees from above. He saw kids running across the lush grass and playing on the treehouse and slide. While the Enclave kids laughed out loud, a few of the Blue Mountain Base kids were still hesitant, with haunted looks etched on their faces.

It would fade. Niko curled his hand into a fist. He'd make sure of it.

Near the fenced-off vegetable-garden beds, he saw long tables loaded with food, and on one, a giant cake with multiple tiers. His people in the kitchens were doing their best to welcome their new members, and he was grateful for it. Music was piped in through hidden speakers, and he suspected once the party got moving—and the beer and wine were flowing—there'd be dancing.

He wanted to dance with Mackenna, her small, toned body pressed against his. He let out a breath. But he may have misstepped there. By firing a shot across her bow, he'd given her a warning, and he was certain she'd pull out all the stops to ward him off.

Well, for the moment, he planned to break down a few other barriers. He approached the kids.

"Niko!"

A few Enclave children crowded around him. He saw some Blue Mountain Base kids hanging back. He pulled something out of his pockets.

"I've got new trading cards for you." He handed the closest kids a card each, all of them cheering and jostling.

"Cool!" A boy spun and held his card up. "I got Marcus Steele."

"Well, I got Roth Masters," a girl announced proudly.

The kids showed off the small cards Niko had sketched. He'd first started the trading cards after they'd moved to the Enclave, using sporting teams that no longer existed and sporting heroes who were now long dead. A way to remember and honor the past.

This time, he'd done a card for each soldier in the squads. The images were sketched in simple black and white, the soldiers' names and squads scrawled at the bottom.

"So cool." A little girl in a pretty pink dress held up one of the Squad Nine ladies.

Niko caught the gazes of the hovering Blue Mountain kids. He jerked his head and they didn't need a second invitation.

"May I have a Hell Squad one, please?"

The thin, young boy's hesitant, polite request was an arrow to Niko's heart. He handed one over. The boy stared at Gabe Jackson's stoic face and a smile broke out.

"Gabe rescued me from the raptors. He's my hero." The boy pressed the card to his chest. "Thank you."

Niko nodded, his throat tight.

The other children crowded close—the bad memories and suffering gone, just for a moment.

"Have you got Reed from Hell Squad?"

"I want a Squad Nine one."

"No, I want a badass berserker one!" a young boy in worn jeans and a faded shirt cried. "I want Hemi."

"Badass is a naughty word," another girl said primly, her blue gaze meeting Niko's. "I want Tane. Please."

Niko handed out the cards he had and finally shooed the kids off to play. Seeing the Blue Mountain children skip away with smiles made his night.

He only had one card left. He held it up, staring at Mackenna's sharp features and tough face. He tucked it back into his pocket. That card was his.

He turned and spotted a few squad members coming in. The berserkers sauntered in—with their worn jeans, torn-off sleeves, and tattooed biceps—

and Niko watched some nearby people edge away from them. They certainly made an impression. When they headed for the bar, Niko wasn't surprised. He saw Roth with his arm around his woman, Avery. Some of the Squad Nine ladies were with them. Where was Mackenna?

Niko turned his head toward the doorway...and his breath caught in his chest.

There she was.

In a damn dress.

Mackenna Carides in her carbon fiber armor worked for him on every level. Mackenna in a dress—a short one that showed off slim, strong legs—left him speechless.

The dress was a bronze color that was the same shade as her eyes. There were no frills or embellishments, just a sleek column of fabric, with thin straps that crossed over toned shoulders and bared slim, but muscular arms.

She'd left her black hair loose, and the color and texture of it fascinated him. God, he wanted to run his hands through it. He shoved them into his pockets to stop from striding up to her and fisting the strands in his hands.

He'd never had a self-control problem before. In his previous life, his control had been vital to his survival. Now he needed it in order to keep his people safe. But something about Mackenna made it all melt away and left him feeling like a caveman.

Even with her hair framing her face, it didn't soften her features. She still had that same tough look on her face. Niko was desperate to see beneath it. He knew that Mackenna had tough in her veins, but there was another side to her. He'd gotten the faintest glimpse of it over the last couple of weeks. The way she savored her food at every meal, the way she snuck into the Garden in her spare time to smell the flowers. She kept a part of herself hidden. He wanted desperately to see that part of her, as well as the oh-so-competent soldier.

For the last two years, Niko had put the needs of others ahead of his own. Sure, he still had his art, that little thing that was his alone. It was his coping mechanism in the chaos. But for the most part, he shoved the other things he needed—the things the man in him needed—down deep and helped the Enclave members thrive as best they could.

He suspected Mackenna did much the same. She kept her needs buried under her armor and her carbine. It was so ingrained that she didn't ever let those inner needs see the light of day.

But now Niko wanted one thing. One woman. More than he'd wanted anything before.

And he was going to do whatever he needed to do to get her.

***

Mac was mad she'd let Cam bully her into a dress. She fought the urge to tug at the hem.

She looked around the Garden and tried to appreciate the ambience. It sure beat sloshing around in raptor muck, or being on the run with no time to relax. The lights in the trees were pretty, and the music was something she recognized, but hadn't heard since the invasion.

She heard laughter, talking, kids giggling. Normal sounds. She felt a little bit of tension leave her. When was the last time she'd really turned off?

Mac swiped a hand through her hair—which was loose. Taylor had forced her to leave it down. This evening, all her squad mates had turned awfully bossy. Sienna had even slipped a condom into Mac's palm and told her to have some fun.

Of course, Mac had tossed it into her bedside drawer. She had a still-functioning contraceptive implant. Not that she planned to use it or the condom, but they were in pretty short supply these days.

The Garden looked nice, but a part of her preferred it at night, when everyone was sleeping. That hushed peace and tranquility.

Mac squared her shoulders. Like she'd told Niko, she couldn't afford to let her guard down. Any second, the emergency siren could blare and her squad could be called out. She could never let herself forget that the aliens were out there. She looked again at the happy, chatting crowd. She couldn't forget she was one of the only things standing between these people and death.

She was just about to make her way over to Roth and the others, when she felt someone watching her. She stiffened. She knew without turning who it would be.

Dammit. She felt a rush of heat on her skin. Trying to stop herself—and losing—she turned her head.

Niko stood near the trees, illuminated by the twinkle of fairy lights. Mac drew in a sharp breath. He wore dark jeans that hugged him perfectly, and a white button-down shirt that looked so good against his bronze skin. He stood with that fluid ease, a man in tune with his body. Those green eyes were on her—dark and intense—and her chest felt tight.

She turned away and walked quickly over to her squad. "I need a beer."

Cam shoved a bottle at her. "Mac, you look bangable. If I didn't like penises..."

Roth and Theron were used to Cam and neither reacted. Taylor snorted, Sienna giggled, and from nearby, Shaw, who was busy stroking Claudia's back, hooted out a laugh.

"Don't any of you encourage her." Mac took a sip of her drink, and the moment the golden fluid hit her tongue, she stopped and groaned. "This isn't homebrew."

Cam shook her head. "It's the real deal. They've pulled out all the good stuff for this party."

Good food and drink had always been high on the list of Mac's secret little obsessions. Beer, wine, spirits, she didn't mind anything, as long as it was the good stuff. On her R and R, she used to blow a fair bit of her pay on the best restaurants, and buying good food from the fine-food markets.

She'd been making do with the homebrewed ale

that passed for beer at Blue Mountain Base...but this was honest-to-God Corona in a bottle.

"And I have a glass of chardonnay." Taylor lifted her glass and took a delicate sip. The woman looked like a beauty queen...but she was one who could kick butt. She shivered and smiled with a moan of appreciation. From nearby, several men's gazes sharpened on the woman.

"Wait until you see the food." Sienna, the final member of their squad stood beside Theron, who towered over the curvy brunette. "So. Good. They have outdone themselves for this little shindig. My mama couldn't have cooked up a better spread."

And Sienna's Italian mother had apparently prided herself on her cooking.

Mac's mouth watered. Okay, now she was itching to try the food. None of her squad mates had ever noticed that she had a fetish for the finer things in life. While you were on the run and fighting invading aliens, it was pretty damn easy to hide.

"I'm going to check it out." With a wave, she headed for the loaded food tables. When she spotted Camembert cheese beside some home-baked crackers, she almost wept. On the next platter, there was some kind of cured ham and a crumbling goat's cheese, which gave her vague memories of her Greek mother. Before she'd died, Mac's mother had always put a bowl of feta out for every meal. Mac's gaze zeroed in on the desserts—chocolate cake, little tarts, and, *oh, God*, there was a huge bowl of raspberries. Fresh, juicy, and piled high.

Mac filled a plate and moved away to stand beside one of the trees. It was a Eucalyptus, and she could smell the refreshing scent in the air. She tasted some of the cheese and bit back a moan. She tried a little bit of a pasta salad, savoring the taste of the strong balsamic vinegar. And the raspberries...okay, apparently she'd died and gone to heaven. Delicious.

As she took another bite of a red raspberry, she sensed a presence behind her. She went still. She could feel the heat of him against her back, knew he was only an inch away.

"I could watch your face all night as you enjoy your food."

Niko's voice, with that sexy trace of Russian in it, made her set her plate down on a nearby table.

He leaned closer. "You smell so good, Mackenna."

Dammit. She'd indulged with her last pot of gardenia-scented cream, taking her time, rubbing it on her skin. No one else had noticed the smell of it. Why did he have to be so observant?

She wasn't entirely sure what it was about Nikolai that worried her so much. She just knew, deep down in her gut, that she needed to stay away from him.

"Dance with me?" he murmured.

She looked over to where a small number of couples were now swaying to the music beneath the trees. "I don't think so."

"You rush out to fight aliens every day without flinching, but you're too afraid of me to have one dance."

She spun. God, he towered over her. She was used to that, but it didn't mean she had to like it. "I am not afraid of you."

Niko cocked his head. The light did fantastic things to his face. It was lean, not-quite-handsome, but definitely masculine. It made Mac think of fallen angels. The dark, wicked kind.

"Okay. You're afraid of what's between us."

She hissed out a breath. "There is no *us*, Niko. I barely know you." God, but she remembered the first time she'd seen him. When she'd pressed a gun to the back of his head.

"Prove it. Dance with me." He held out a hand.

Mac had never been one to back down from a challenge. She and her brothers had always been daring each other, and it was a matter of pride to always follow through. She stared at his hand and saw faint streaks of white and blue paint. She wasn't sure why, but she found that sexy as hell. She liked that he left it there, uncaring what people thought of it.

She looked around and saw Cam, Taylor, and Sienna doing wild contortions in her direction. Well, Cam was. Taylor was making a "go on" motion with her hand, and Sienna was rubbing her hands together.

God, if she didn't dance with him, her squad mates would never let her live it down. "One dance." With a loud huff, she put her hand in his.

ANNA HACKETT

She ignored the electric tingle of his skin against hers and fought the savage urge to snatch her hand back.

With a slow smile, Niko pulled her closer to the dance area.

Once they reached the other couples swaying under the lights, Niko swung her into his arms. Mac caught a glimpse of a few female faces in the crowd watching them. None of them looked pleased about their most eligible bachelor being otherwise occupied.

Mac held herself stiff at first, but slowly the easy sway, the hard body, and the beat of the music made her unwind a little.

One dance wasn't anything to worry about.

"You enjoyed the food?"

She nodded. "You have lots of things we didn't."

"We have extensive stockpiled supplies and an experimental protein replicator. Not quite the same as real steak or chicken, but it's close." He smiled. "We don't always break out our best rations. Tonight is special."

As they moved to the music, she tried not to let herself relax too much. But it was hard. His hand slid down to settle in the small of her back, the brush of their bodies was intoxicating. "You're a good dancer." Her voice had the tiniest hitch.

"My Russian blood. My parents both loved to dance."

There'd been no dancing in her family. Mac was sure her grizzled father had never even danced at his wedding.

Niko pulled her closer, her cheek pressing against his chest. "Just stop thinking," he murmured.

It couldn't hurt, could it? Just for a little bit? She breathed in that citrus-lime scent of him and closed her eyes.

They kept swaying, and he murmured something in Russian. Mac just let herself feel, cracking open that love of sensation. It all flooded in, the faint taste of the raspberries, the warm feel of Niko and his strong arms around her, the scent of him and the trees, the sound of the music and the steady beat of his heart under her ear.

"Mackenna." His lips brushed over her ear.

She shivered, desire a slowly unfurling coil of heat in her lower belly. What would his hands feel like scraping over her skin? What would it be like to unbutton that shirt and explore his lean body?

"God, you drive me crazy," he said against her hair. "I want to touch you, taste you." One of his hands slid down the outside of her thigh, fiddling with the hem of her dress.

For a bright second, she wanted to drive him even crazier. "Where would you touch me?"

She felt his chest hitch. "I'd start at the bottom. Your slim ankles, your slender legs." He rubbed the skin of her thigh in a circle. "I'd like to taste the inside of your thighs. For all your tough shell, I bet your skin is so soft."

God. She squeezed her eyelids closed. "What else?" *She did not just say that!*

"I'd slip my fingers under your panties. I want to

see how wet you are for me." His tone had turned husky, the Russian accent deeper.

Mac licked her lips. She couldn't believe she was doing this. "I would be."

He muttered what had to be a curse in Russian. "You are an evil woman."

She felt the hard bulge of his erection against her stomach. She was teasing herself as much as him. "What else?"

"I am hungry to know how many fingers I can fit inside you."

She jerked against him. *God*.

"How swollen your clit gets when you're turned on."

A beeping noise broke through the sensual haze. She heard Niko mutter a curse, his hands flexing on her. Then, reluctantly, he released her and pulled a small communicator from his pocket.

He looked at the screen and his face went hard, all desire leaking away. "Emergency meeting in the Command Center."

Mac looked over and saw Roth waving them over.

Locking her knees and ignoring the throb between her thighs, she hurried over, Niko at her side. "What's going on?"

Roth's face was like stone. "A message from Lia. They lost a drone an hour ago. Close to the alien ship at Sydney airport."

Mac frowned. "Malfunction?"

Niko shook his head. "No. Her message says she just lost a second one...in the same area. She was still getting some feed from them, then they disappeared off screen."

Mac's stomach turned over. "One could be a malfunction, but two…"

Niko nodded toward the doors. "Two means we have a massive problem. Let's get to the Command Center."

Chapter Four

Niko paced in front of the screens in the Command Center as Lia spoke.

The head of the drone team was trying to conceal her panic, but it was written all over her pretty face. "The drones both went down in a similar location. We lost the visual feed first, then we lost the ability to control them."

"But you could still track them?" Niko asked.

She nodded. "They were both still moving, like something was transporting them—" she swallowed "—toward Sydney Airport."

Toward the raptors' main base.

If the raptors had discovered a way to detect and capture the drones it would be a nightmare. "And you can definitely rule out a malfunction?"

Noah Kim stepped forward. "They were both serviced recently. Were in perfect working condition when we sent them out today."

"You lost the feed off one yesterday, right?" Mackenna said. "Then it crashed into a tree. Right here near the Enclave."

Lia nodded. "Mac and Cam recovered it. It looks like that one was a malfunction."

Niko didn't like this at all. He caught Adam

Holmes' gaze and saw that the general looked worried, too.

Holmes straightened. "The drones are vital, not only to our plan to fight back against the aliens, but to our survival."

Niko thought of the squads, of Mackenna, heading out to face the raptors with no intel and no support...they'd be going in blind.

Nyet. No way. "We need to get these two drones back, and work out what the hell is going on."

Lia cleared her throat. "One is completely off grid. I have no idea where it is. The other is giving an intermittent signal, and it doesn't appear to be moving." She turned to a screen and a map flashed up. "It's in a park area on the Georges River, just south of Bankstown."

Niko ran a hand through his hair. Far too close to the aliens' mothership at Sydney Airport.

Lia frowned at the map. "If the signal is correct, it's in an old electrical substation in the middle of parkland by the river."

Everyone looked grim-faced. Holmes nodded and looked at Roth. "Squad Nine, go in and recover the drone. In and out. Don't announce to the aliens that you're there. Do not engage." He gave Roth a hard look. "Unless you have no choice."

Niko watched Roth, Mackenna, and the rest of Squad Nine leave at a jog. He watched until the door closed, hiding Mackenna from view.

Soon, he stood beside Holmes, staring at a video screen, as the now-armored and armed Squad Nine moved into the Enclave hangar. They'd had limited vehicles before, but now the space was home to the small fleet of Hawks and the Darkswifts—two-man, stealth gliders that he'd heard Squad Nine liked to use.

He watched Roth waving his team onto a Hawk.

Niko watched Mackenna leap aboard. Funny, he found her just as attractive dressed in her armor as he had in her dress. Soon, the rotors started, and a moment later, the Hawk lifted a few inches from the hangar floor. Above, the overhead doors retracted, and the Hawk disappeared from view.

They picked up the drone feed now. Niko imagined the small drone, somewhere in the air above the Enclave, zeroing in on the Hawk. He watched the Hawk reach altitude, tilt, and aim north toward Sydney. The drone followed it for a bit before stopping, and the Hawk got smaller and smaller on the screen.

Holmes was standing stiff and tense beside him.

."It's hard watching your people go out?" Niko asked.

The older man gave a nod. "I thought it might get easier over time, but it never does." Piercing blue eyes looked Niko's way. "You'll have to get used to it, if we're going to fight hard enough to drive the aliens away."

Niko nodded. As a leader and as someone who'd once fought for his country, he understood that. He understood sacrifice. But as a man...he looked back at the image of the Hawk. As a man, it was damn hard to watch the woman you had yet to touch or taste fly off into danger.

He released a slow breath. If Mackenna knew he wanted to keep her safe, she'd kick his ass.

Another screen flared to life, and now they could see the feed coming in from a camera attached to Roth's combat helmet. It showed the members of the squad sitting calm and composed, checking their weapons.

Niko didn't like how damn close they'd be to the raptors' main base. "Any raptors in the vicinity of the downed drone?" he asked Arden.

The cool comms officer didn't even turn around, her hands tapping at the screen in front of her. "Nothing on sensors. The park where the substation is located is heavily forested. That might keep them away from the area."

Yes, the raptors' dislike of trees was a hotly discussed topic. But their brazen assault on Blue Mountain Base proved it wasn't a foolproof defense.

As the Hawk drew closer to the target, Niko felt his muscles getting tighter and tighter. He had sent his security teams out around the Enclave many times. But watching a team head into the ruins of Sydney, right on top of the aliens, was a different story.

"Starting descent now." The smooth male voice belonged to the Hawk pilot, Finn.

Niko saw Mac move close to the side door, one hand gripping the handhold above her head.

The next second, the Hawk's skids touched down.

"Go, go." Roth waved them out.

The door of the Hawk slid open, and the camera

bounced as Roth and his team leaped to the ground.

Niko got an impression of trees, the curve of the river, and then Squad Nine fell into formation, weapons up, as they jogged down a path.

"Four hundred meters ahead on your current heading," Arden said.

Niko leaned a hip against the desk, and tapped his fingers on the surface. It was his one weakness when he was nervous. He always needed something to do with his hands.

The squad moved out of the trees, and directly ahead lay the substation. It was large, covered in metal towers with wires strung between them. It had probably been partly derelict long before the Gizzida had arrived. Many places had switched to the small nuclear power plants after small-scale nuclear power had been made safe, along with a mix of solar power.

"Theron, open the gate." Roth's quiet murmur came over the line.

The big, quiet man moved forward, pulling a tool off his belt. Niko saw the flare of a laser cutter as the man went to work cutting open the wire gate. Around him, the remaining squad members fanned out, carbines up, ready for anything.

Niko's gaze fell on Mackenna. God, that tough face. It was hard to believe that not that long ago, she'd been standing in his arms wearing a sexy little dress and driving him out of his mind.

Now she was in danger, risking her life for them all. It just made Niko want her more.

The gate squeaked open, and Squad Nine moved forward, Mackenna in the lead.

"Go straight ahead another twenty meters," Arden said. "Then turn right, then left around a transformer. You should see the drone somewhere nearby. That's where the signal's coming from." Arden's fingers flew across her screen. "Lia said to keep a lookout for it anywhere. It might even be stuck on the wires overhead."

"Any of this live?" Camryn asked. "I really don't want to get zapped."

"Most of the substation was shut down long before the invasion. After the invasion, any remaining power into it would have been cut off. There's a chance something might still be active, although nothing is showing on my screen."

"Okay Nine, let's not get fried," Roth said. "Don't touch anything."

"I see something," Mackenna said.

Niko leaned forward and saw Adam do the same. They watched Mackenna turn the corner around a large metal tower Niko guessed was the transformer.

He saw it the same time she did. Ahead, lying on the ground, he saw the twisted remains of the drone.

Mackenna knelt. Roth stood over her, capturing a perfect view as her gloved hand touched the mangled metal.

"Shit," Mackenna said. "It's partly melted. Something did a number on it."

Niko watched as she pulled out a black mesh

bag and shook it out with one hand. She carefully lifted the remnants of the small quadcopter drone into it. She clipped the bag onto a belt.

"Got it."

"All right, Nine," Roth said. "Let's get out of here. Way too quiet around here."

In formation, they started out of the substation. Niko thought the whole place looked pretty eerie, with the combination of skeletal towers and derelict structures, and damaged wires hanging down from above.

Suddenly, Niko saw Arden stiffen.

"Roth, I've picked up heat signatures heading your way! They came out of the river."

"Raptors?" Roth's voice carried an edge.

"Yes," Arden answered. "A full patrol, by the looks of it. Get out of there."

The squad picked up the pace, but as they neared the gate, the raptor patrol was almost on them.

Holmes leaned down close to Arden so his voice carried to Squad Nine. "Do not engage. Roth, if you can, find an alternate exit, or hide and let them pass."

Chyort voz'mi! Niko drummed his fingers on the table. They were too fucking close to the raptor base. If this patrol spotted them, they'd call in reinforcements. They'd rain down on Squad Nine, and there'd be no way to help them.

"Take cover," Roth said.

The men and women fanned out, each of them finding a spot to squeeze in to and hide behind.

From where Roth was crouched behind some metalwork, Niko had a perfect view of Mackenna. She was crouched low beside a big wooden spool that held what looked like old wiring.

He also had a perfect view of the humanoid raptors coming in through the gate. They were big bastards, with scaly skin, hellish teeth, and burning red eyes. They carried large, scaled weapons and wore some sort of metallic armor on the lower halves of their bodies. They'd stopped, and were grunting over the cut-open gate.

The raptors moved together as a group, looking around, and searching the area.

Niko gripped the edge of the desk, his fingers pushing hard against the wood. He'd been on missions like this one in his past life. Plenty of times, he'd had to hide and avoid detection. He'd been renowned for his patience, his ability to blend in and wait out his enemy.

But watching someone else do it, someone he felt that early stir of feelings for, made him feel damn helpless.

He saw a big raptor wandering toward Mackenna's hiding place. *Nyet.*

Niko drew a breath. Held it. *Turn around, you bastard.*

He saw Mackenna peek around the reel she was using for cover, taking note of the raptor. She swung her carbine onto her shoulder.

Niko frowned. "What the hell is she doing?"

"Stay calm, Nikolai," Holmes said. "She knows what she's doing."

He watched Mackenna draw a large Gladius combat knife out of the sheath strapped to her thigh.

"She's going to engage." Fear was a solid punch to Niko's chest. "She'll get herself killed!"

Holmes didn't bat an eyelid. "She's an experienced soldier. She'll do what she needs to do."

Niko fought to take a breath. If she moved, she might find better cover and stay hidden. Engaging was suicide.

The raptor turned the corner around the spool. Mackenna stood, spun, and thrust her knife into the raptor's chest. As he fell, she followed him, slammed her gloved hand against his mouth. God, if the alien got any of those razor-sharp teeth into her, he'd tear her hand apart. He was jerking his head and her hand muffled his snarl.

He hit the ground with a thud, Mackenna kneeling on his chest, her body blocking their view.

Niko took a second to admire her work. She was good. Damn good.

But if any of the other raptors had heard, they were still in danger.

And once they realized they were missing one of their soldiers...

Roth shot forward and together he and Mac grabbed the creature's arms and dragged him behind the transformer. Hiding him from view of his comrades.

Arden was murmuring quietly into her earpiece.

Roth spoke in a whisper. "Nine, alternate route

to the east. Follow me."

Roth's team moved like stealthy wraiths through the substation. Soon, they reached the side fence, and once again, Theron cut a small hole through it. The team slipped through the gap and into the trees.

"Arden, confirm Finn is in position for our pickup," Roth said. "We're on our way back."

"He's touching down now, Roth," the comms officer answered. She slumped back in her chair. "See you when you get back."

Niko released his death grip on the table. But it wasn't until he saw the entire squad climb aboard the waiting Hawk, and the Hawk shoot up into the air, that he finally took a deep breath.

He willed himself to relax. To let the tight muscles across his shoulders loosen. To not keep replaying over and over that scene of Mackenna taking on the monstrous raptor while an entire group of aliens was right nearby.

She was on her way home. That was all that mattered.

Chapter Five

Mac jumped out of the Hawk and into the hangar, slinging her carbine over her shoulder.

The rest of her squad disembarked and the Hawk's rotors started slowing down. Right now, she was thinking about the mangled, melted piece of metal in the bag attached to her hip. She didn't know what the hell had happened to the drone, but whatever it was, it wasn't good.

She saw General Holmes and Nikolai stride into the hangar, and tried to stay relaxed. Now was not the time to think about that sinfully sexy dance they'd shared.

Besides, the tight look on Niko's face didn't remind her of the sexy man she'd danced with. His gaze brushed over her, and she saw his jaw was clenched tight.

"Well done, Squad Nine," Holmes said.

Mac held the bag out to him.

"Thanks, Mackenna. I'll make sure this gets to Lia, Noah, and the tech team. Hopefully we'll have some answers soon."

Roth nodded. "Let's hope the raptors just got lucky. Maybe it was nothing."

And maybe this entire invasion was just a bad

dream. Maybe she'd wake up tomorrow in her pretty little apartment, messages from her dad and her brothers on her voicemail, while she pondered what decadent thing to make herself for dinner.

Niko was practically vibrating with tension. "Your team always take risks like this?"

Mac's spine went stiff. What the hell? She looked up and saw Niko was staring straight at Roth.

Roth raised his eyebrows. "Risks like what?"

Now, Niko's gaze turned on her, his eyes blazing. "Like jumping a raptor twice your size and risking giving away your position. Your position— and the positions of your teammates—while you are right near a fucking base filled with raptors."

Anger—hot and molten—stormed through Mac. Oh, no, he couldn't be doing this.

Niko wasn't finished. "If you'd moved, found another hiding spot, or just held your location —"

"He would've stepped on me." The fury made it hard for her to get the words out. No one questioned her judgment in the field, except her direct commander. "And that would have put my team at greater risk. You weren't there, Ivanov. We go out there every day to fight. Don't pretend you know me, or know what it's like."

She turned and stormed off. She couldn't even put into words how angry she was right now. She'd dealt with plenty of macho alpha males. Ones who'd wanted to tell her how to do her job, tell her that she couldn't possibly have the chops to make it in this kind of work.

She was damn good at her job. And she knew it.

And Mac knew the pain slicing through her heart right now had nothing to do with her confidence about herself. It had to do with the fact that the man she was attracted to had just questioned her abilities.

Dammit. She strode down the corridor, ripping off her chest armor as she went. She was disappointed. She stopped in the squad locker room, stomped up to her locker, and tore it open. She tossed her gear inside and forced herself to take a few calming breaths.

Nope. She didn't feel any calmer. She'd thought, just for a second, Niko was different. That he respected her abilities.

Without letting herself think, she stalked down the corridor to her new apartment. She moved inside, barely taking note of the pretty, pale-green walls and the big double bed—both of which were far nicer than the bare concrete walls and narrow bunk she'd had at Blue Mountain Base. She continued right into her adjoining bathroom, savagely controlling her thoughts. She flicked the shower on and pulled the rest of her gear off. When she stepped under the hot spray of water, she tried to stop the thoughts from coming.

But as the water poured down over her, she finally let her shoulders sag.

Damn the man. She'd liked him. And by not trusting her judgment and doing his bit of chest beating, he'd hurt her.

She'd known this would happen. That's why she'd tried to stay well clear of him in the first place. She couldn't afford to be the soft, pretty plaything men seemed to like. She wasn't that woman and she never would be. If he didn't like that, that was too bad.

When she felt a slight stinging in her eyes, she turned her face up to the water. *No way. Suck it up, Mac.* She was going to put Niko Ivanov and their brief flirtation behind her.

She was going to do what she did best. Her job.

***

"You really put your foot in it yesterday."

Niko looked up from his sketchbook and leaned back in his chair. Cam McNabb was standing in front of him, a short skirt showing off her long, long legs, her hands on her hips.

If he sketched her, he'd make her an Amazonian warrior, spear in hand.

He looked back down at his sketchbook. He was sitting in the main dining room, doing some simple charcoal work. Everyone had finished breakfast, and he liked the feeling of space in the large room. It was something he often missed, living underground.

He didn't need Cam to tell him that he'd screwed up. He knew, and he was mad at his own idiocy.

"I know." It was a gruff rumble.

He'd let the unfamiliar and new feelings of fear and concern for a woman cloud his judgment. He knew Mac was good at her job, and that she didn't need him telling her what to do.

55

She didn't really need him at all, and maybe that was the problem.

Cam sighed and dropped into the chair beside him. "You want a chance with Mac?"

He looked up at the other woman. He nodded.

"Well, you fucked up. Big time."

The sense of finality in her words made his heart stutter.

"But...she does look at you differently," Cam continued.

He lifted his gaze and kept it steady.

Cam smiled, but it wasn't nice. "Well, at least she did. She's never paid any attention to men, but when you aren't watching, she watches you."

Really? So far, Niko felt like he'd been doing all the chasing, and not getting very far.

Cam's gaze narrowed. "Don't look so pleased with yourself. She'll have all her defenses up now. And that woman has a hell of a defensive network. You'll really have to sweet-talk her."

Sweet-talk tough, no-nonsense Mackenna?

Cam crossed her legs. "She's one of the best damn soldiers I've ever worked with. Whatever the challenge, she wades right in and gives it everything she's got. She's tough. She's loyal. And she's determined. But she never lets herself just enjoy. That woman is always switched on."

"I think her off switch is rusty." That was exactly what Niko noticed. He could see how much she'd been enjoying the different foods at the party, but she'd been hiding her reaction from everybody. She had the same look on her face whether she was in carbon fiber, climbing into a Hawk, or attending a party. Like she never truly relaxed.

Cam laughed for a second before her face turned serious again. "Her father sounded like a tough bastard. Never spoiled her, just treated her like another son. Her mom died young, so she didn't really have a feminine influence in her life. She told me she never got to have any nice things."

"She likes good food. I think she has a sweet tooth."

Cam gave him a considering look. "Good eyes, artist man. Now be smart."

As Cam sauntered away, Niko turned the page in his sketchbook. He stopped on a page showing a sketch he'd done of Mackenna in her armor. He traced a finger down the paper, then he tore it out and folded it in two. He was a good strategist. He was sure he could come up with a plan for wooing the woman.

He glanced at his watch. He had a Command Center meeting in ten minutes to hear an update on the drone they'd recovered.

He tucked his sketchbook under his arm, made a short detour past the kitchen, and then went on to Mackenna's room. He slipped the sketch under her door and tied his other gift to the door handle. Then he walked quickly to the Command Center.

When he pushed open the door, he saw the others were already there. Mackenna was standing beside Roth. She glanced his way, but looked right through him.

Chyort, that hurt. And he had no one to blame but himself.

When Noah saw he'd arrived, the tech man tapped a keyboard. "Now we're all here." Images of the damaged drone filled the screens. "I'll share what we've got so far. The drone was virtually destroyed. Something attacked it and tore it open, and parts of it were also melted."

"Raptor poison?" someone asked.

Noah shook his head. "The lab is still running tests. It isn't the same as the raptor poison we usually encounter, but they also can't rule out that it is some other sort of raptor poison."

Niko blew out a breath. That wasn't very helpful.

Noah went on. "We really don't know what happened to the drone. Whether it was deliberately targeted or hit by accident. We managed to get some footage off the drone's internal memory. There's not much."

One screen filled with shaky footage. The drone was moving at a good pace, showing an image of the ground below and a little bit of the sky ahead.

Then something shot past in front of the drone. Too fast to make it out, it was no more than a dark shadow. Niko squinted. What the hell was that?

Then, a second later, something slammed into the drone from above, making it shudder and start a spiral drop toward the ground. The sizzling of something burning through metal could be heard.

From next to Noah, Lia kicked the leg of the desk. She looked pissed.

"Something took it down," Marcus said in his gravelly voice.

"There's no way they can detect the drones," Lia said. "They have illusion systems on them. There's no way the aliens can see them."

"Maybe they have new tech?" Noah suggested. "I know we'd prefer that wasn't the case, but we have to consider it."

"Maybe they just got lucky," Lia countered.

Niko scratched the back of his neck. From the unhappy silence and the tension in the room, he knew none of them believed that.

"General?" Niko looked at Adam. "Your suggestions?"

Holmes shook his head. "I don't see that there is any more we can do right now. We keep a close eye on the drones, and if we have any more incidences..."

The man didn't need to finish that sentence. Everybody knew the answer.

If the aliens had found a way to take down their drones, they were screwed.

**

Mac found the chocolates tied to the handle of her door.

She untied them and opened the packet. She breathed deep and, not letting herself think too hard about it, popped one in her mouth. The flavor of fresh raspberries and dark chocolate exploded against her tongue.

She pushed open her door and ate another chocolate. They were exquisite, and she was going to eat them, but she wasn't softening. She knew exactly who'd left the little peace offering on her door.

She wasn't interested.

She spotted the folded paper on the floor. She picked it up, tempted to look at it. Instead, she dropped it on her table.

It took a couple of minutes to change into her training gear and grab her gym bag. Before she walked out, she stopped. She stalked back to the table and opened the paper.

She'd expected a note. Instead, an image of herself looked up at her. She stared at it for a long moment, then dropped it back on the table. *Damn you, Niko.*

She headed toward the gym. She had a date with two hot guys, and she planned to take out her frustration on them.

On the way, she spotted a group of kids huddled together in the corridor. She recognized a few of the children from Blue Mountain Base, and was pleased to see them making friends and laughing. Just being kids.

"Hey. What's happening?" She stopped beside them.

"We're trading cards," a boy told her with a grin. He held up a card.

It was a perfect picture of Roth looking tough and badass.

"You have others?" she asked.

All the kids pushed forward to show her. She saw Cam, Taylor, Sienna...all looking like the strong, brave soldiers they were. Her throat tightened. "Where do you get them?"

"Niko makes them." A pretty girl smiled. "Aren't they cool? I want to be on Squad Nine when I'm bigger."

"They are very cool." Mac ran her hand over the girl's hair. Leaving the kids to it, she kept heading to the gym. And every step of the way, Niko dominated her thoughts.

Gabe and Shaw were waiting for her when she arrived. As she stepped into the gym, she took a second to once again admire the place. Blue Mountain Base's gym had been pretty basic—a big space with some scavenged weights, treadmills, and mats for sparring.

The gym at the Enclave had been specially designed, and equipped with the best. High-tech equipment lined the back wall that was covered in mirrors. The top-of-the-line free weights were off to the other side. And in the center was the sparring area, with a few private sparring rooms off the side. There was also a squash court, basketball court, and the indoor pool.

She started across the mats toward the two men waiting for her. Big, intimidating Gabe and long, lanky Shaw. Doc Emerson and Claudia Frost were two lucky ladies.

Best of all, as far as Mac could tell, both these men didn't just respect the abilities of their women, they supported them as they did their jobs.

Mac dumped her bag and started stretching her neck and arms. "I'm looking forward to our session today, gents."

Shaw groaned. "That means you're in a bad mood and you're going to take it out on us."

Mac shot him a little smile. "You're pretty smart for a sniper." She sank into her fight position.

Across from her, the men did the same. *Game on.*

They'd sparred together plenty of times. Both of them tested Mac in different ways. Gabe was big and strong. Incredibly strong. She'd heard whispers that he'd been in some top-secret Army super-soldier project before the invasion. She didn't doubt it for a second.

Shaw was smart and sneaky. As a sniper, hand-to-hand combat wasn't his specialty, but he was good and he was fast. The biggest thing he had going for him was the fact that he could read his opponent very well. A few times, he'd anticipated her moves and tossed her onto the mat.

Mac rushed at Gabe and launched into a series of attacks. He blocked them and got in a few bone-jarring hits of his own. Mac managed to flip Shaw twice before he got mad and found his rhythm. But for the most part, she got in more than her fair share of hits. She tried not to feel guilty about taking her frustration with a very different man out on these two soldiers.

She tossed Shaw over her shoulder and he landed flat on his back on the mats with a groan.

"I'm waving the white flag, Carides," he panted.

"Damn, you are mean."

Mac circled around Gabe, and the man matched her movements, watching her steadily with his gray eyes.

He lunged in a few times, but Mac didn't fall for the bluffs. She watched him, cataloging every little shift of his feet, and waited to see any sort of tell on his face.

There. The slightest shift of his eyes. As he moved in, she dodged around, got in a good chop to his thigh. When he stumbled, she grabbed his arm, swiveled, and they went down.

Gabe hit the mat with a heavy thud, and Mac landed beside him with her knee pressed to his chest.

He gave a short nod. Coming from Gabe, that was pretty high praise.

Shaw gave another groan. "I'm out of here. I'm gonna let my woman put my pride back together."

Gabe snorted. "You know she's going to tease you."

Shaw grinned. "Probably, but then she'll get me naked, so it'll be worth it."

Mac stood and started stretching. "Go. I don't want to hear the details of your sex life."

Shaw waggled his eyebrows. "If you have anything to share, I'd like to hear it. But as far as I know, you don't have a sex life."

"And if I did, it would be none of your business, Baird."

He held his hands up in mock surrender. "I'm not sure any man's brave enough to get close to you. You'd just toss him on his head."

Shaw's words stung. She shrugged a shoulder. The one man who she'd thought she wanted close...well, she wouldn't mind the chance to toss him on his head.

Gabe and Shaw left with casual waves. Mac still felt an edgy tension running through her body. Maybe she should run it off on the treadmill.

That's when she glimpsed a movement out of the corner of her eye. She saw Niko emerge from a shadowed corner of the gym.

Chapter Six

Had he been there the whole time? Mac was angry with herself for not noticing him. That kind of lapse could get her killed in the field. "You're good at hiding."

"Old skills." He walked closer with that easy, loose-hipped stride, paint streaks on his shirt.

She hated that her pulse leaped at the sight of him. But more curiously, she heard the dark undertone to his words. Old skills apparently also came with old scars.

"I got the chocolates," she said.

He came closer. "Did you like them?"

"Sure."

He moved his hand, holding out a pretty flower with creamy-white petals. "I'm sorry, Mackenna."

Stay strong. She didn't say anything. She hadn't expected the outright and honest-sounding apology.

"Seeing you out there…I know how good you are, but I had this visceral reaction to watching you in action, in danger."

Mac turned away and gave him her back. He came up behind her, his body brushing hers.

"I don't want to see you hurt." He stroked his hand and the flower down her arm. "I don't want to see this body hurt. I haven't even had the chance to touch it yet."

She felt herself melting, wavering. She wasn't going to do this.

She turned and aimed a fist at his stomach.

He moved faster than she thought possible and blocked her, catching her fist in his palm.

Her gaze narrowed. She tried another strike. He blocked that one, too.

This time Mac launched a full-on assault. Kicks, hits, blows. She drove him back across the mat. Every move she made, he blocked with a skill and expertise that stole her breath.

Just what the hell had he done before the invasion?

Testing him, she pulled out some of her best moves backed by all her strength. Hit to the stomach. Chop to the arm. Kick to his side.

He blocked every move. And never once made an offensive move back.

"I'm not going to fight you, Mackenna."

She aimed a kick at his chest. He gripped her ankle, stopping her foot an inch from hitting him. He held her there, her leg extended up.

"What if I want you to fight me?" Her blood was surging.

He released her. "No."

"You think I can't protect myself?" She punched out and he knocked her hand away. "You think I'm not a good soldier?" This time she got a good kick to his gut before he dodged her foot. "You think I can't handle whatever it is you've got?"

Angry now, she launched herself at him. She landed against his chest, wrapping her legs around him. They spun in an ungainly circle. She leaped off, and while he was unbalanced, she gripped his arm and flipped him over her shoulder.

He went down, but before she could pin him to the mats, he jumped up without using his hands. A brilliant display of strength and speed.

"I know you're good," he said, his face serious. "I didn't mean to make you doubt that."

"I don't doubt it," she bit off. "But I don't play with men who don't respect me."

She attacked him again. But before her foot connected, she saw something change in his face.

His patience snapped.

He launched back at her. He grabbed her around the waist, lifted her, and slammed her down onto the mat.

The air rushed out of her lungs, and she lay there, shocked, for a second. She rolled and jumped to her feet. He backed her across the mats and she struck back a few times—hit, kick, block.

Mac's breath hitched and she had to put everything she had into warding him off. Next thing she knew, he grabbed her, and flipped her onto the mat.

She landed flat on her back. She was trying to roll away when the next thing she knew, he was lowering his body over hers.

Mac blinked. No one, not Roth, not Gabe, not Shaw, none of the soldiers she trained with, had ever pinned her to the mats.

"I respect your fucking abilities. Didn't you see the drawing I left you?"

He'd made her look strong but feminine. She wasn't sure how she felt about it. "Yes. And I saw some of your trading cards."

He smiled. "You liked them."

"I didn't see one for me."

His smile widened. "That one belongs to me."

Mac shook her head. "Niko, you could have your pick of women around here. I've seen the way they watch you."

"I've never wanted any of them the way I want you."

"You and I make no sense. I'm a soldier, you're a leader."

His lips lowered close to her mouth. His gaze ran over her face. "It doesn't have to make sense. But to me, it feels damn right."

He kissed her.

The taste of him flooded her—he'd tried one of her chocolates, and tasted of hunger, raspberries, and sin. The kiss was a tangle of tongues and teeth, and he growled into her mouth. She fisted a hand in his thick, silky hair and pulled him closer.

The sudden blare of a siren made them wrench apart. Both of them were breathing heavily.

Her short-circuited brain started firing. It was the alarm for the squads. "I have to go."

He pushed off her, then gripped her hand and helped her to her feet. They stood there for a second, looking at each other. Then he slid a hand into her hair, pulling her face up to his, but stopped short of kissing her again. "Be careful."

She waited for more. For the demands, the orders, the ultimatums.

When he said nothing else, she nodded. "I'll see you when I get back."

He leaned down and grabbed the flower he'd dropped. It had somehow survived their fight. He handed it to her. "Count on it."

***

Niko couldn't stop himself from heading to the Command Center. He knew Squad Nine had gone into the field to save a small band of human survivors who needed help.

As he walked in, he could hear Arden talking in her calm voice. But there was an urgency underlying it. Holmes stood with his hands behind his back, watching the screens intently.

On the screen, Niko watched the Hawk lower toward the ground. On the stretch of road below, he could see humans in three beaten-up vehicles, under attack by raptors.

"We're going in hot, Nine. Let's do this." Roth sounded like he was talking about them going out to play a game of basketball.

Niko knew the squad was good, but it didn't stop him from worrying.

He saw Mackenna and the others leap off the quadcopter. The feed was a chaotic blur of laser fire, frightened shouting, and the deep grunts of the aliens. Niko locked down his emotions. The woman he wanted was a soldier. He had to deal with that.

He saw the way the squad tore into the aliens. Mac and Cam were covering the humans where they huddled near a car. Roth led the rest of them to take down the attackers.

The squad worked together well—anticipating each other, backing each other up.

They were magic.

"Another raptor patrol incoming. They're one klick away." Arden tapped on her screen. "Come in, Lia. I need a drone redirected out to the north of Squad Nine's current location. I need more details on these incoming raptors."

"On it," Lia's voice came across the speaker.

Suddenly, Niko heard a high-pitched growl cut across the lines. His head snapped up. What was that?

He heard Mackenna's curses, then her frantic voice. "Roth! The humans we're helping...they are raptor hybrids. I repeat, raptor hybrids. It's a trap."

"They're armed," Cam shouted.

Nyet. Niko stared at the screen. Beside him, he heard Holmes mutter a sharp curse.

Lia's new drone appeared, giving them clear images. The feed made Niko's stomach clench. He could see now that the humans that were right near Mac and Cam were actually hybrids. Humans who'd had their DNA altered and alien DNA added. Some had scaled patches on their faces, others had red eyes, and others had claws on the ends of their hands.

Arden shot out of her chair. "Lia, I've lost the feed from drone one. Can you get it back?"

Niko spotted the now-black screen.

An expulsion of breath on the speaker. "I'm not sure what's wrong with it. My people are working on it—"

Niko watched as the feed on another screen blinked out. *What the hell?*

"We've lost another one," Holmes said.

"I need the feed to see the incoming raptor patrol," Arden shouted. "I need it back!"

The final screen went blank.

Niko could still hear the screams and grunts. He could still hear swearing from the Squad Nine soldiers.

Then he heard Roth's voice. "What's that in the sky? Shoot it! Shoot it now."

"Roth," Arden said. "We've lost visuals on the drone feed. If we lose—"

Suddenly the sound cut off. Silence.

Arden sat back and pressed a hand to her mouth. "We've lost everything."

His gut rolling, Niko moved forward. "What the hell do you mean?"

The door slammed open and Lia raced in. She stared at the screens with horror. "We have no feed in Squad Nine's area."

Niko's heart was hammering against his chest. They were blind.

Holmes reached forward and grabbed the mic on Arden's desk. "Roth, abort. Get back here." There was no response. "Do you copy? Abort!"

71

Silence.

Niko spun to face Arden. "Hell Squad. Get them out there to help. Now!"

Holmes gave a sharp nod, and the comms officer frantically tapped at her screen.

Niko stared up at the blank screens. *God, Mackenna, be okay.*

***

Niko paced in the Hawk hangar.

"They're fine," Holmes said from nearby.

Niko knew Hell Squad had made it out and rescued Squad Nine. They were all on the way back in.

But he wasn't going to feel any sense of relief until he saw them. Saw her.

An alarm sounded as the overhead doors retracted. A second later, he saw the shadow of the Hawk lowering.

Its skids touched down, and the side door slammed open. Marcus leaped off, followed by the rest of Hell Squad. Niko shifted impatiently. Then Squad Nine exited.

When he saw Mackenna, covered in blood and gore but unhurt, Niko finally released a breath.

He wanted to touch her, quite desperately. But he was filled with a volatile emotion he'd never felt before. Hell, in his previous work, he'd been known for having ice in his veins.

Right now, he was more volcano than ice floe.

He saw her talking with Roth, and then she

pressed her hand to her leader's arm and nodded.

She was alive. Niko turned around and stalked out of the hangar. He needed to contain this emotion before he approached her. He didn't want to risk saying the wrong thing to her again.

He needed his paints or his clay.

He strode through the corridors and ended up in the Enclave library. He had a small corner set up like a studio.

Thankfully, no one else was in there. He only had the rows of books for company. It was a lovely spot, lots of warm wood, and deep, burgundy leather chairs. Usually, the space soothed him and let him be creative.

Right now, it did nothing to soften the jagged edges inside him.

On the wall was one of his paintings. It was a wild, chaotic picture he'd done not long after they'd moved to the Enclave. A representation of his life before, the violence of his past.

He stepped in front of his easel, uncapped his paints, and set to work. This would be no pretty, delicate painting. It would be much like the one on the wall. Maybe the violence of his past really wasn't as gone as he would have liked.

A little while later, he sensed her.

Breathing deeply, he spun, holding up his paintbrush like a sword. She'd taken her upper armor off, but still wore it from the waist down. Her dark-green T-shirt stuck to her body, outlining the sweet shape of her breasts.

They stared at each other across the space.

"I made it back okay." She walked closer, but he could sense she was wary.

With rigid control, Niko put his brush down.

Mackenna stopped just a few meters away. With a growl, he moved toward her and scooped her up. As his mouth crashed down on hers, he backed her up against the shelves.

Her hands clung to his shoulders, and she kissed him back.

He swept his tongue into her mouth, and she met him halfway. Her hands moved to cup his cheeks, her tongue dueling with his. He pushed deeper, needing the taste of her, the connection.

She made a hungry noise, her hands moving again, sliding up under his shirt. Niko felt wild, untamed. He was filled with want, need, desire. All for her. As he pushed against her harder, a book fell off the shelf and thudded onto the floor. He ignored it.

He shoved up her shirt now, and pushed the fabric of her sensible sports bra out of the way. He pulled her upward and clamped his mouth down over one of her nipples. He sucked on her and loved her small, wild cry.

"The door's...open," she panted.

Niko didn't give a crap.

But he moved his lips back up, nipping at her neck before taking her mouth once again.

Then he heard a tinny noise. A voice. With a frown, he finally managed to drag his mouth from hers. Her head was tilted, and he realized the voice he heard was in her earpiece.

She licked her lips and it made him groan. He pushed his hips forward so his bulging cock pressed against her.

Something flared in her eyes, but she kept her hands on his shoulders. "That was Arden. We both need to go to a meeting in the Command Center. To discuss what we found out on the mission."

Niko pressed his face to her hair and breathed deep. He nodded. Sometimes being in charge sucked.

Then he felt Mackenna's hand stroke his cheek. "I really am okay, Niko."

He dragged in a breath, smelling her scent. That faint perfume of lush flowers mixed with the sweet smell of sweat. Alive.

He stepped back. "We'd better go."

Chapter Seven

By the time they neared the Command Center, Mac almost had her wild desire under control, but there was still a hot trickle in her veins. She hadn't felt attraction like this for so long, and now she was wild for one man.

As she and Niko pushed through the doors, she felt her squad mates watching her. She refused to make eye contact with any of them.

"What have we got?" Niko asked.

Lia pointed at a screen. There was a blurry image on it and Mac squinted. It looked vaguely birdlike, and the same as the brief flash of what she'd seen in the sky on the mission.

It had been pretty touch-and-go—hybrids rushing at them, raptors firing, and something flying in the air overhead, taking out the drones.

"What is it?" Niko asked.

"We're not entirely sure yet," Holmes answered.

Lia cleared her throat. "It looks like some sort of bird of prey. Whatever this thing is, it's a drone killer. It's either some sort of device or alien, and it's targeting our drones."

"We managed to track where this drone killer has taken the last few drones it's destroyed." This time it was Elle Milton who spoke. "It keeps heading toward Sydney Airport."

"The alien ship?" Marcus asked.

"Nearby. There's an industrial area that's made up of old fuel tanks. For some reason, the drone killer is taking the drones it destroys back there."

Holmes stepped forward. "We need to find out what it is, and we need to know how to defeat it."

From beside the general, Niko shoved his hands on his hips and scanned the room, his face serious. "If we're ever going to take these aliens down and drive them off our damn planet, we need the drones. They are vital to providing our intel and to keeping everybody safe—the squads and the civilians. We need a plan."

As Niko started discussing ideas with General Holmes, Marcus and the other squad leaders, Mac sensed her squad members flanking her.

"That man is so damn sexy," Sienna murmured.

"Must be that hot Russian blood," Taylor said. "I bet the man can kiss."

"Forget that," Cam said with a drawl. "I bet that man has a big cock."

Mac made a choking noise and glared at her friends. "Hello? Debrief and planning a mission here."

"Oh?" Cam said. "So, you want to tell me why you look like you've been kissing somebody? Your hair is all messed up."

Mac instantly raised a hand to smooth over her hair, and immediately realized there was nothing wrong with it. She glared at Cam, but her friend was already giving her a "gotcha" look.

"Ladies? Anything you want to add to this?" Niko asked.

Mac straightened. "No."

Cam turned with a smile, cocking one hip. "Please, go on."

Niko tapped his fingers against the desk in front of him. "General Holmes and I are agreed. We need a team to sneak into the drone killer's home area. We need any and all information we can get on it." He sighed. "But we have a big problem."

Mac crossed her arms over her chest. She knew exactly what the problem was. "Whoever goes in will have no drone support. It'll be a blind mission right into the heart of alien territory."

Silence fell around the room.

It was a suicide mission.

***

Niko scanned the tough, determined soldiers around him. He knew this was going to be a dangerous mission, but none of them looked concerned.

"This mission will be all about stealth," Holmes said. "The team needs to get in and out quietly."

"We need anyone with advanced recon and covert operations experience," Niko added. "We cannot afford to be found anywhere this close to the alien base. They find us, we die."

"I'll go," Mackenna said.

Niko pulled in a breath. He'd suspected she'd

volunteer, but that didn't mean he liked it.

Roth nodded. "She's my best at stealth, and she'll provide good firepower, in case you need it."

"Let's hope we don't need it," Niko replied. He saw her watching him, waiting for what he'd say. She was waiting for him to disappoint her again. He traded a look with Holmes, then nodded. "You're in."

Her face didn't change, but he sensed her relief.

"Gabe," Marcus said.

The big man gave one single nod. Niko had no doubt that Gabe would be excellent on this mission.

"Count me in." A crisp, English-accented voice. "I've been in the area a few times, so I can help."

The words came from Devlin Gray. Niko still had trouble believing the man who looked like he'd stepped out of the pages of *GQ* magazine was also good at sneaking into alien territory. But he was Santha Kade's right-hand man on the intel team, and everyone said Devlin Gray was beyond good.

Holmes inclined his head. "I'd hoped you'd say that, Devlin."

Niko nodded. "And I'll be going. The general and I agreed that we should keep the team small. Four will be good."

He saw Mackenna's head shoot up, her eyes widening. "You?"

Hell Squad's Shaw spoke. "Aren't you an artist?"

Niko didn't look at the man, he just kept his gaze on Mackenna. This wasn't how he'd wanted to tell her about his previous life. Hell, he didn't want to tell anybody. He'd worked so hard to put his past behind him and had hoped to leave it there.

"Before I came to Australia...I worked for Russian Intelligence."

A hush fell over the room.

He dragged in a deep breath. "I was part of a specialized unit."

"What unit?" Mackenna demanded.

He paused. "Zaslon."

"Zaslon was a myth, a rumor," Elle said quietly.

"No." Marcus' gravelly voice. "They weren't. I've seen some of their agents once. They were ghosts."

"You were an assassin," Mackenna said.

Her face was so carefully blank he suspected she was never going to look at him the same way again. "I can get in and out of this location better than any of you." Stealth had been his skill. That...and killing.

Mackenna shook her head. "You're out of practice. You've been here in the Enclave for almost two years, and before that, you were out of the field for however long. Besides, you're a leader here, you're important..."

Niko saw everyone turn and stare at her. "My life is no more important than anyone else's." A lesson he'd learned the hard way. "I can do this."

"I think I can vouch for him." This time it was Avery Stillman, Roth's partner, who spoke. "When I was with Coalition Central Intelligence, we had a very thick file on a shadowy Russian agent simply called Nikolai." Her gaze met his. "I've connected some dots."

"Nikolai is a common Russian name," Niko said.

But there were loud gasps around the room. This was the one secret he'd hoped never to reveal. He looked at Mackenna and saw a mix of emotion on her face—shock and horror were the loudest of all.

"You're *the* Nikolai," she said.

Shit. He inclined his head. Yeah, he guessed it wasn't much fun to find out the man you'd been lusting after was a deadly agent and assassin with the most confirmed number of kills in intelligence history.

Most days, he could barely live with it himself.

He cleared his throat. "We leave tonight at 03:00. I suggest those of you on the team get prepared, get some rest, and be ready to leave."

Niko left the room without looking back.

***

Mac tried to sleep. But after two hours of tossing and turning, her sheets tangled around her legs, she gave up.

She had all her gear ready for the mission, but she felt edgy and tense. She thought about heading to the gym and beating something up, but instead, she found herself heading to the tunnel leading up to the Garden.

When she walked into the garden area, she instantly felt her muscles relax. Moonlight filtered down from above into the silent space, and the smell of grass and leaves hit her.

Mac kicked off her shoes and walked out onto

the grass. It was soft and cool under her feet. It was then she realized that she didn't have the place to herself.

Frozen, she stood there watching him. He had an easel set up and was painting wild, bold strokes. His jeans hung low on his hips, and his white shirt was undone, baring a hard, bronzed chest. His feet were bare like hers, and for some reason, she found that outrageously sexy.

She was conflicted about his past. She was a soldier, she'd killed, but always in the heat of battle. She wasn't sure how she felt about an assassin who snuck in and took lives in the shadows. How could she reconcile the man she was getting to know, this man in front of her right now, with what she'd learned? Steady, sexy hands, the creative artist, the natural leader...and now she had to add ruthless assassin.

Mac pulled in a breath. A lot of people had been something else before the alien invasion. So much had changed, and so many people had changed with it. None of them were who they were before.

When she looked up, she saw that he was watching her. She walked over to him.

"I...should've told you before," he said.

She stopped. "I knew you weren't always an artist. I figured you had some military experience, so I can't say I was too surprised."

"But you're a woman who sees in black and white, Mackenna." He gave her a sad smile. "I like that about you. No shades of gray. I'm very gray."

She moved around so she could see his painting.

It was a splatter of bright, bold colors all melding together. "I've never thought you were gray, Niko."

It took her a second to realize that the bold lines and colors were her face. He'd made her look somehow exotic, beautiful, beyond the ordinary. "I don't look like that."

He smiled. "You do to me."

"I don't want you on this mission," she said baldly. "I don't care if you were a super assassin before."

"I don't want you on the mission, either, so we're even."

She let out a frustrated breath. "Niko."

"I don't care about the mission right now. I care about knowing if you can deal with my past."

Mac shoved a hand through her hair. "I know a lot of people aren't who they were before. I guess we'll just have and see."

"Do you want me to touch you again?"

God, the depth of pain in his voice flayed her. She couldn't be anything less than honest with him. "Yes."

He sat on the small stool near the easel, then he reached out, and in one of those quick moves of his, pulled her into his lap. His lips brushed over hers in a featherlight caress. Almost like he was afraid to kiss her.

"I wish we weren't heading into danger in just a few hours." He fiddled with the buttons on her shirt. "I wish we had all the time in the world. I could get you out of your clothes." He flicked one button open, stroking the skin at the base of her neck.

She swallowed, heat making her legs feel weak.

His tone lowered and his accent thickened. "I wonder what your skin tastes like. At that pulse point on your neck, on your belly, behind your knee. I wonder how your clit would feel against my tongue."

Mac felt something inside her spasm. Oh, that dark, sexy voice whispering those dirty things to her...

"I wonder how my cock will stretch you, Mackenna. What noises you'll make as I fill you."

"You'd better fucking stay safe on this mission," she said, "or you'll never find out."

He went still. "When we get back, you'll let me have you?"

"You'll have to come back to find out."

He slid his hand into her hair, tugging her head back. "We're both coming back safely."

She heard the promise in his voice. But she'd been on enough missions to know things went wrong. She looked around the quiet, deserted garden. There was no one around. And maybe it was time she let loose some of the things she kept hidden inside her.

"Well, we'll see when we come back. But right now, you could find out how my clit feels in your mouth."

She felt his muscles bunch beneath her. He made a deep growling sound. Before she could think, he scooped her up and moved deeper into the trees. A second later, her back hit the grass.

Mackenna couldn't get enough air in her lungs. He was looming over her, and then he knelt, tugging at her trousers. He stripped her with a methodical intensity that made it hard to breathe.

"I'm not tame or patient, Mackenna." His palms slid along her legs. "Right now, I'm very hungry."

He reached out and grabbed a flower off a nearby bush. It was a wild, pink bloom—full and lush. He undid the buttons on her shirt and flicked it open. She wasn't wearing a bra. He made a sound, running the bloom down her cheek, down her neck, across her breasts. The petals were as soft as silk on her skin and she arched up into the sensation. She could feel the grass beneath her, smell the beautiful, lush scent of the flowers, and she could smell him—sexy, hungry man.

He dragged the bloom down her legs, teasing the sensitive skin on the inside of her thighs. With a growl, he tossed the flower away, gripped her legs, and pushed them apart. He wasted no time leaning down and then his mouth was on her.

Mac reared up. The shock of wet heat was so good.

He lapped at her. Long licks up and down. Then he found her clit, circling it. *Oh.* She tried to hold on to some sanity, but he gave her no chance to assimilate the sharp, bright feelings battering at her. His tongue was a wicked weapon and it didn't matter what else was happening, she just wanted to come.

He sucked her clit between his lips and she

shattered with a thin cry.

As Mac came back down, Niko was pressing kisses against her thighs. She felt his hand slide up to cup one of her breasts, thumbing her nipple lazily. She looked down and saw he was smiling.

"You look pleased with yourself," she said.

"Hell, yeah." He dragged his fingers over her skin, down her belly. "Plus I had paint on my hands." His smile widened. "Now you're covered in streaks of it."

She looked down and gasped. The imprints of his fingers were caught in paint on her breasts, streaks on her thighs, on her belly.

He pressed his palm against her quivering belly. "Don't wash these off." He reached up and cupped her breasts again. "I want to be on this mission and know my marks are on you. Our sexy little secret."

"Niko—" If any of the squad saw them, she'd never live it down.

"My marks are all over you." He dragged a finger over her belly. "My claim."

She sucked in a breath. Sinful, sexy man. She wasn't surprised he wanted to claim her...what surprised her was that she liked the idea. Did that make her weak? Stupid? She wasn't sure, but she knew she wasn't washing the marks off before they headed into danger.

Chapter Eight

It was different seeing it with your own eyes.

Niko stood in the Hawk, holding on to an overhead handhold, and staring out the side window. Dawn was still a ways off, and the world was lit with only a murky, gray light. But it was enough for him to see the devastation below. He knew what the shattered ruins of Sydney looked like. He'd seen them on the screens numerous times before.

But this was his first time flying over them and seeing it for himself.

As the Hawk swept northward, Niko took in the broken towns, the abandoned cars, the overgrown fields. *Damn aliens*. It made him more determined to make this mission a success.

The carbon fiber armor felt familiar. As did the well-used knives he still cleaned and cared for that were tucked inside his armor. It was as if the years he'd put between him and his previous job were gone in an instant. There wasn't much he missed about his previous life, but that sense of anticipation before a mission...nothing quite matched it.

He looked behind him and spotted Gabe leaning

against the back wall of the Hawk. Devlin Gray sat relaxed in a seat, somehow looking suave and stylish in his armor. Mac sat behind Devlin, calmly checking her carbine and laser pistol.

The sight of her made Niko's heart clench. Okay, one thing might exceed the feeling of heading out on a mission. Stripping Mackenna Carides naked and putting his mouth on her. He let his gaze drift down her body, hidden by the black carbon fiber, but he knew his marks were there.

Chyort, he was getting hard. At that moment, she lifted her head and their gazes caught. He saw the heat flare in her eyes. She knew exactly what he was thinking.

Soon, they reached the outskirts of Sydney. The devastation was much worse here. His jaw went tight. The crumpled and burned-out houses, the partly-collapsed office buildings and shops. His hand clenched on the handle.

At the Enclave, they'd stayed hidden away and safe. While they'd done that, so many had suffered and died.

Mackenna moved up beside him. "It's hard to see, isn't it?"

So many dead. The words echoed in Niko's head. "Yeah."

"There's the airport," she said with a nod of her head. "And the ship."

Niko hissed out a breath. Lights were on around it, illuminating the huge leviathan. The aliens' giant ship looked like a hulking sea creature. Monstrous and terrifying.

"I've seen it before," she said, "but this will be the closest I've ever gotten to it. Hell Squad, Reed's fiancé, Natalya, Roth, and Devlin had a mission to infiltrate it and retrieve some alien energy cubes."

The thought of her anywhere near, let alone inside the alien ship, made Niko break out in a sweat.

"Okay, listen up," Dev said from behind them. "This drone killer's territory is just past the alien ship, near the water. Finn will drop us as close as he can get us, a few kilometers away, and we'll go in from there. Full stealth mode. We get to the location, scope it out, and see what we can see."

"Don't go in the water," Gabe said.

"Why?" Niko swiveled.

Gabe shrugged. "Believe me, you don't want to know. But it has a lot of teeth."

Brilliant. Niko looked back out the window and felt the Hawk begin its descent.

"In position," Finn called back from the cockpit. "I can't risk getting any closer. You need an evac, you need to get back to this point. I'll be hiding out and waiting for you."

Gabe shoved the door open. They were hovering a few feet off the ground. He watched Mackenna leap out with practiced ease. He followed her, pulling his carbine into his chest.

Once Gabe and Dev were out, they watched the camouflaged Hawk pull away.

They were in the heart of alien territory, with no comms to the outside world.

They were on their own.

The four of them fell into position. Crouched low and staying close together, they moved forward. Dev took the lead.

"We need to head that way." Dev pointed across the mass of runways that had once served Sydney.

They raced forward, using patches of long grass for cover. In between the runways, the grass was tangled and overgrown, while the runways themselves were cracked and buckled.

As they waded through another patch of grass, Niko thought about the creature the squads called the velox—a cunning ambush predator resembling velociraptors. It didn't sound like anything they wanted to run into.

Suddenly, Dev held up a hand. They all dropped down to the ground. Niko pushed aside some grass in front of him and caught a glimpse of a raptor patrol ahead.

"Wait them out," Dev murmured.

Beside Niko, he saw Mac watching the scene with her cool, tough face. So damn sexy.

They waited and finally the raptors moved on. Their team headed off again. Niko spotted a lot of activity in the distance, by the alien ship. But in the quiet corner where they were, there didn't appear to be much going on. Niko looked up and scanned the slowly lightening sky, looking for that shadow they'd seen on the drone feed. *Nothing*.

Soon, a cluster of large, squat tanks appeared out of the shadows ahead. He guessed they'd been used for fuel.

"Look." Mackenna pointed.

As they got closer, he saw that some of the tanks were rusted, with a few holes visible in them here and there. But on top of the one on the far right, where Mackenna was pointing, he saw a strange collection of branches, leaves, and trash perched on top.

What the hell?

Dev nodded and they made their way over to the tank. They circled around it and Niko spotted the ladder attached to the side.

Dev went first, then Mackenna, and then Niko. Gabe brought up the rear.

They climbed onto the tank's flat roof and Niko sucked in a breath.

It was a nest.

The drone killer had made it out of whatever the hell it had scavenged. In the center of the huge nest, he spotted bones—bleached white by the sun—fast-food wrappers, bits of plastics, foil, and cardboard, and pieces of electronics.

"There's the drone," Mackenna said.

Or what was left of it. The thing was in pieces.

"I'll get some shots." Dev pulled out a tiny camera. He wasted no time getting images of the nest.

Niko saw Gabe looking upward and he did the same. Yeah, Niko was pretty sure they didn't want the drone killer to find them standing in the middle of its nest.

"Mac, grab the drone," Dev said.

With a nod, Mackenna pulled open a bag and moved forward. She started scooping up the remnants of the drone.

Suddenly, Gabe crouched by the edge of the tank and lifted his carbine. "Down. Raptors."

They all crouched and Niko swiveled. He looked over toward the alien ship and spotted a patrol of raptors, their lights arcing ahead of them as they patrolled.

"Hopefully they'll go the other way," Makenna whispered.

They all stayed frozen, tense. Mackenna's shoulder brushed against Niko's and he willed the raptors to head in the opposite direction.

Suddenly, there was a groan of metal beneath them.

Chyort voz'mi! Niko felt the metal beneath them bowing under them.

"Shit," Mackenna whispered harshly. "It's giving way!"

Niko reached out and wrapped his arm around Mackenna. A second later, the metal beneath them gave out.

He heard her curse and then they were all falling down into the tank.

***

Fuck. Mackenna pushed to her feet. Nothing was broken or hurting. "Everyone okay?"

Gabe and Niko were already standing, but Dev was sitting up, cradling one arm. He probed the limb and looked up.

"Broke my arm."

Mac felt her stomach clench. *Double fuck.* Outside the tank, she could hear the guttural shouts and grunts as the raptors came closer.

"We're sitting ducks in here." The raptors had to have heard the collapse. All they had to do was climb the tank, aim their weapons down, and open fire. Mac knew they'd be dead in seconds.

Gabe was circling the tank like a caged lion. He stopped at a hatch at the back. He slammed his shoulder against it and the entire tank shuddered.

Mac hurried over, Niko at her side. "You think you can get it open?"

Gabe gave a single nod. "I'm gonna try."

Gabe started slamming against the hatch. Mac arched her neck, looking all around. She spotted a few weak spots in the metal, showing the brightening sky behind...but they were all well above their heads. Why couldn't the damn thing be rusted down here at the bottom?

She watched as Gabe hammered his body against the metal, his muscles straining. It was clear he had enhanced strength, but right now, even that wasn't enough against the inches of thick steel.

"Raptors are getting closer." Niko's tone was grim.

Like her, he was looking up, staring at the metal walls of the tank.

Then he swung his carbine around. "I'll climb up. Try to buy some time for Gabe to punch through the metal."

Climb up? Mac looked at the tank's slick sides

askance. "You can't climb this. There's nothing to hold on to. You'll never make it."

"I've climbed things far harder than this."

Her heart started hammering against her ribs. "Even if you could climb out, you can't take on an entire raptor patrol alone."

"I can if it buys you time."

Her chest spasmed. "Niko—"

He grabbed the front of her armor and yanked her close. The kiss was hard. Short. Not enough.

He turned around, pressed his hands against the metal, and started climbing.

Hell, the man was like a spider. He kept a smooth, steady pace, somehow finding the smallest things to hold on to. If it had been her, she'd have slid back down a hundred times.

Clearly, being a former assassin meant he had some interesting skills.

She wanted to call him back, but bit down on her tongue. She'd told him that he needed to respect her abilities and her work. She had to do the same for him.

He reached the top of the tank and paused, but never looked back. Seconds later, he disappeared over the edge.

Mac looked back at Gabe. "Get the hatch open." She moved closer, trying to find a way to help.

Gabe grunted and kept ramming his shoulder against the metal. She saw a growing dent in the metal, but the hatch still hadn't given way.

Devlin stood nearby, watching intently, keeping his arm still.

With nothing left to do, she moved over to him. "Let's get this arm strapped."

She pulled out her field first aid kit. She grabbed a bandage and fashioned a sling. She made sure she didn't focus on the bit of bone she saw protruding through Dev's armor. That the guy wasn't screaming or hadn't passed out from the pain was a miracle.

She looked at his face. The guy was outrageously handsome, with an elegant, sexy edge that gave a woman fantasies. "How come some woman hasn't snapped you up yet?"

He gave her a faint smile. "Guess I haven't met the one, yet."

She finished wrapping his arm. "I bet the Enclave beauties are tripping over themselves."

Another quirk of his lips. "I'm quite...choosy."

"That, I believe."

"So, you and Nikolai, huh?"

She didn't answer, but instead, raised her head, listening. Wondering again what he was doing outside, and if he was staying safe.

Dev tilted his chin. "It's kind of obvious when you two look at each other."

Outside the tank, she heard a sudden burst of carbine fire. It was met by the distinctive sound of raptor weapons.

Mac's fingers curled into fists, and she closed her eyes.

"Don't count him out," Dev said. "He was a hell of an agent. People used to whisper about him in the halls of every covert agency around the world.

He can take care of himself."

Mac managed to nod. But Niko was going up against aliens—big, strong, ruthless aliens. An entire patrol of them. And he was alone.

She heard the groan of metal and turned back to Gabe. The hatch was distorted and bent out of shape. He was getting closer to breaking through.

Then the gunfire outside cut off.

Her pulse skipped a beat. God, what had happened? Was he okay?

She swung her carbine around and aimed it upward. She hated that she was stuck in here, helpless.

She heard a voice shouting. Russian cursing.

She swung back to Gabe. "They have him! Gabe—"

"Almost there." Gabe banged his shoulder one more time. Then the big man swiveled and pressed his palms against metal and pushed.

Screw this. Mac couldn't stand here and do nothing. She moved close to Gabe, pressed her palms beside his and pushed.

They strained hard. Mac felt her muscles burning. She had to get to Niko.

Suddenly, the hatch gave way. They stumbled forward as the circle of metal fell out onto the ground.

Mac wasted no time throwing her leg through the narrow gap and climbing out.

Ahead, on the nearby runway, she spotted Niko fighting the raptors.

Several aliens were down, their bodies

motionless on the ground. But there were still lots of them on their feet, circling around Niko's smaller form.

He was fighting with one raptor. Heavy kicks, hard hits. The man could fight.

But she could see Niko's face was swollen and bloody on one side. The alien was getting in his own blows. Even with his armor on, Niko would be feeling the pain of each strike.

He dropped down, slamming into the raptor's knee. The alien toppled, and Niko sprung on top of it, shoving forward with a hand.

Knives. Niko was holding knives in each hand.

"Come on!" Mac called to Gabe and Dev.

The men were climbing out of the tank. Dev was holding his gun with his left hand and looked comfortable doing it. Gabe was right behind him.

She turned...just in time to see a giant raptor slam a fist into Niko's face. *No!* She winced, watching Niko fall to the ground.

Niko pushed up onto his knees, but she could see he was dazed. She started running.

One of the aliens spun around with a snarl. He slammed a huge fist into Niko's body.

Niko flew sideways, and landed on his side. All the remaining raptors surrounded him, kicking him with their giant boots. Blow after heavy blow to his stomach, chest and face.

God, no. She lifted her carbine, pushing for more speed.

Chapter Nine

Every breath burned.

Niko was barely holding onto consciousness. *Nyet. Got to keep fighting. Got to give Mackenna and the others time to get away.*

He fought to stay conscious, but pain was a living, breathing thing clawing at his insides. Mackenna fought for everyone else, day after day. This time, he was fighting for her.

He struggled up and a hard punch of a clawed fist sent him down again. Vicious kicks hammered into his gut and chest. He felt ribs break and gave an agonized shout. He tasted blood in his mouth.

Gritting his teeth, he rolled over and managed to strike out and knock one raptor over.

He pulled out his knives. Even after all these years, they were a familiar weight in his hands. In this moment, he was glad for his skills. Glad he could kill as many of these aliens to keep Mackenna safe.

Niko swiveled, barely containing a groan, and threw the knives. The blades lodged in the lead raptor's throat. The creature grabbed at them, stumbling backward.

Another vicious kick landed in Niko's lower

back. He sprawled forward onto the ground. He clawed at the dirt, rolling as fast as he could... *Get up, Ivanov, or you're dead.*

He looked up to see the final raptor standing above him, his ugly, scaled weapon pointed straight at Niko's head.

He didn't have time to think, or plan, or watch his life flash before his eyes. It was just a single image of Mackenna that filled his mind.

Laser fire cut through the air. It tore into the raptor's body and the alien jerked. He toppled forward, and Niko barely managed to roll out of the way.

Using the last of his strength, Niko pushed to his knees. He swayed and realized he couldn't go any farther. He stayed there, trying to fight through the fog of pain growing in his head.

"Niko!" Mackenna skidded to her knees in front of him.

Gabe and Devlin were right behind her. Even with his right arm in a sling, Dev was firing a laser pistol with impressive precision. Gabe moved around, checking the downed raptors. Any that were still breathing, he took care of with a double tap of his carbine.

Mackenna touched Niko's swelling face. "Goddammit, Niko."

She probed his wounds, making him wince. "You made it out."

She cupped his cheek. "And you let them beat you up."

He smiled, then felt his lip split. "Sorry."

She checked him over with sensible no-nonsense pats. When she reached his abdomen, she hissed out a breath. "Their kicks got through your armor."

He nodded. "Ribs are broken. Pretty sure there's some internal bleeding."

Her touch turned soothing now. "I have plans for this body, damn you."

He kept his gaze on hers. "That hurts more than what they did."

She looked up at Gabe and Devlin. "He's hurt bad. We need to get him to medical help ASAP."

"We can't call it in," Dev reminded them. "We'll have to get him back to the evac point."

Kilometers away. Niko swallowed back the taste of blood and bile.

"Need to move," Gabe said. "Have to assume these guys called for reinforcements." He toed one of the raptor bodies.

Mackenna wrapped her arm around Niko, wedging her shoulder into his armpit. "You need to get up, Niko. Up for a stroll?"

His entire body rebelled. "Mackenna, I can't stand up."

Gabe shifted. "We've got incoming raptors. A lot of them."

Dev frowned, following Gabe's gaze. "I don't see or hear anything."

"You will in about two minutes," Gabe said.

Dev shook his head. "You are spooky, Jackson."

Niko willed his body to move. Every move was agony. He took a deep breath, pushing down the gut-wrenching pain and the accompanying sorrow.

It was time to face facts. "You guys need to go."

"No." Mackenna's head whipped around, her tone emphatic.

"I'll slow you down. You have to go, Mackenna. Now."

"Is that your bossy-leader voice?" She raised a brow and dug her shoulder deeper into his side. "Up and at it, Ivanov."

So stubborn. He knew her exoskeleton would be doing a lot of the heavy lifting, but he was still bigger and heavier than she was. He managed to get to his feet, but he was shaky. She was taking the bulk of his weight.

"Okay, just put one foot in front of the other," she said. "Gabe, cover us. Dev, you good shooting left-handed?"

"I'm fine. You just help Niko."

They started moving. Every step was excruciating, and he knew that they were going too slow. He looked ahead, focused on just lifting a boot and setting it down. But he knew he was putting them all at risk.

He tried to focus on the fact that the sun was coming up and bathing everything in a pretty early-morning blush of light. But they hadn't gone far when the pain started to make him nauseous. And the last thing he wanted to do was puke up his guts in front of Mackenna. He felt a laugh burble inside him. Funny that he was more worried about embarrassing himself in front of a woman than the raptors chasing after them.

But the pain had stolen his ability to talk.

Walking was taking everything he had.

"I can carry him," Gabe said after a minute.

Niko scrounged up some energy. "Not fucking carrying me, Jackson." He pushed the words through his gritted teeth.

"I'll help him," Mackenna said quietly, her arm tightening on him. "If it comes to that."

She was already taking most of his weight. "You're not carrying me, either." The thought left him vaguely horrified.

"Then keep moving."

He did, riding through the pain. She started murmuring to him. Quiet encouragement. Praise. Damn, he liked it. Over the last eighteen months, he'd had to listen to more than his share of complaints, fears, concerns. There hadn't been much praise. And before that...well, no one really took the time to congratulate you on being a good killer.

"We're getting closer," she said. "Keep going."

Maybe he could make it. With her help.

"Down!" Gabe cried out suddenly.

Raptor fire tore through the early-morning stillness. Mackenna shoved Niko hard. He hit the ground and the wave of pain that rolled over him made him groan. Sweat broke out on his brow. He was going to be sick.

Nearby, Gabe was busy returning fire and taking down the raptors. Dev was firing, too.

But there were more aliens getting closer. Shouts and grunts filled the air.

"Let's go." Mackenna forced Niko up again,

trying to heave him onto his feet.

"I...can't. I won't be responsible for your death. Go." He'd never been one to give up. But more than anything, Niko wanted her safe.

She got in his face. "You want me naked in your bed?"

Even wracked with pain, he felt a brief surge of heat.

"Hell." Gabe looked away from them.

"You want to do anything and everything to me?" Mackenna said.

Nearby, Devlin let out a short bark of laughter and started whistling.

Niko ignored them. "Yes."

She leaned in close, her nose brushing his, her voice low with a seductive edge. "You want to slide your cock inside me? See how much you can stretch me?"

"More than anything," he whispered.

Her seductive voice disappeared. "Then keep moving, Niko."

This time, it took both Mackenna and Gabe to get him on his feet. They started off again, but he was well aware he was moving even more slowly than before.

"Bribing me with your body," he gritted out.

"Consider it incentive," she answered. "It isn't bribery, if we both want it."

There was a roar of sound. Lights whizzed overhead in the brightening sky.

"Fuck," Mackenna bit out. "Ptero."

"Run!" Dev cried out. "As fast as you can."

Niko saw the raptor ship wheeling about ahead of them, turning to make another pass. It was shaped like a pterodactyl, with fixed, triangular wings. They were fast and deadly.

In front of them, a ptero, and behind them, raptor troops. They were fucked.

Suddenly, a wide spray of laser fire blasted through the air. Niko turned his head and saw the welcome shape of a Hawk appear out of nowhere.

More laser fire tore through the sky, hitting the ptero. But these shots weren't coming from the Hawk.

Mackenna grinned. "My squad."

That's when Niko saw the small, sleek, dark shapes whizzing past at great speed. The Darkswifts.

The Hawk lowered and Gabe jogged up to it and yanked open the side door. With Mackenna and Gabe's help, Niko managed to get aboard. He collapsed onto the floor.

All the sights and sounds seemed to move around in a dizzying swirl. He couldn't focus on anything anymore. He felt a warm hand on his face.

"Hold on. I've got you."

He tried to hold on to her voice, but he couldn't stop himself from passing out.

***

Mac paced in the waiting room outside the Enclave infirmary.

It was plush, lined with comfy chairs, with a coffee machine in the corner. It was nothing like the bare concrete tunnels she'd waited in at the Blue Mountain Base medical center when one of her squad was injured.

But she couldn't use the comfy chairs anyway. She was too edgy to sit, and she couldn't stay still.

Devlin and Niko were still in there. There'd been no news yet. Gabe had gone somewhere to drop off the drone remnants and to update Marcus and Holmes.

It was so damn quiet. Mac had taken her upper armor off and left it stacked beside the wall. She ran her hands up and down her arms and kept up her pacing.

There was a sound at the doorway and she saw Roth and the rest of Squad Nine appear.

"How are they?" Roth asked

Mac felt her lip tremble, and fought to remain composed. She was grateful they were here, but she really didn't want to show any of her worry and concern. "Dev has a broken arm. Niko...he was beaten up." She swallowed. "Really bad."

Cam came closer and slid an arm across Mac's shoulders. "Well, based on Niko's previous employment, and on how in shape that guy is, Doc Emerson will have him patched up in no time."

Mac nodded, but if that was the case, why was there still no word?

Sienna flanked Mac from the other side and patted her arm. Then she peered forward. "Is that paint?"

Cam leaned closer as well. "And here on your shoulder, too?" She grinned. "Did your artist man make you his own private canvas?"

Aw, hell. Luckily, Mac was saved from having to answer when the infirmary door opened.

Dr. Emerson Green stood there in her lab coat. Her blonde hair was mussed and she looked tired, but then she smiled.

Mac shifted her weight from foot to foot. *That had to be good, right?*

"Devlin's fine. I've set his arm and put a regen patch on it. He'll be as good as new tomorrow." Emerson's gaze found Mac. "Mac, Niko's asking for you."

"He's okay?"

"He is now. The nanomeds have done their work. We did have to perform some surgery to stop the internal bleeding, but he's going to be fine." The doctor's brow scrunched. "I have no idea how he walked several kilometers in his condition. It was a miracle he was conscious at all."

Mac nodded and stepped into the infirmary. Inside, it had the typical clean and clinical feel of any medical establishment—white tile floor, rows of beds down one side, and on the other, glassed-in examination rooms. The surgeries and labs were at the back. Members of the medical team were bustling around. It was far larger and better equipped than what they'd had at Blue Mountain Base.

"He's back there." Emerson pointed.

Mac spotted him at the end of the row of beds.

He was sitting up, his shirt on but open.

His green gaze fell on her, intense. "Mackenna."

She walked toward him slowly. She didn't know what to do or say. She was filled with a confusing rush of emotions, and she fought to choke them down.

A soft look crossed over his face. "It's okay to tell me how you feel."

Mac just shook her head. Then, before she thought about it, she climbed onto the bed with him. She wrapped her arms around him and buried her head against his chest.

With a quiet murmur, Niko leaned back against the pillows and pulled her closer.

Mac rubbed her cheek against the warm strength of his chest. She breathed in the scent of him, tinged now with the faint smell of antiseptic.

He lifted a hand and stroked her hair.

"This," he said quietly. "This is what got me back here. If not for you..."

She gripped him harder.

"Doc says my nanomeds are almost finished. And then I believe you promised me a few things."

Mac lifted her head. "Did I?" He had to be feeling better if he was thinking about sex.

His hands tightened on her skin. "You can't back out now."

No, she couldn't, and she certainly didn't want to. "I'm not."

"Good. I want you to go to my room and wait for me there."

That forceful tone of his, his leader voice, left

even more confusing emotions in her. One part annoyance, and one part breathless desire. "Oh?"

"I'll come as soon as I'm finished here." He reached out and tucked a strand of her hair behind her ear. "I want you on my bed, Mackenna. Naked."

Her heart had started a rapid staccato in her chest. "You're using your bossy-leader voice again."

He gripped her hair and gave it a little tug. Then his hand slipped down and traced along her cheekbone. "It's not bossy if we both want it."

"Hello, again." Doc Emerson bustled over, an indulgent look on her face. "Now I see why your heart rate spiked, Nikolai."

Mac bit her lip. "Sorry."

"I'm not," Niko added.

Emerson checked the monitor beside the bed. "It looks like our hero is almost done with these nanomeds."

Mac watched Niko scowl.

"I'm not a hero. Mac and the other squads are the heroes around here."

Both women ignored him.

Mac sat up, and swung her legs over the side of the bed.

"Don't leave on my account," the doctor said.

"It's okay," Niko said. "She has somewhere else to be."

Mac fused her gaze with his. It was her choice now. To take a chance, take what she wanted, and enjoy it.

Or stay locked up and alone.

He watched her steadily, like he knew exactly

what battle was going on inside her.

Then Mac slipped off the bed and walked away. She looked back over her shoulder. "See you soon."

Chapter Ten

Niko hurried toward his room. The nanomeds had done their work, and he felt full of energy. Not just full—he was bursting at the seams, and anxious to get to Mackenna.

Of course, people kept stopping him to chat and check up on him. He tried not to let his impatience show. Finally, he broke free and managed to get to the kitchen, grab the things he wanted, and get to his room.

He paused at his door, and took a calming breath, willing his heart rate to slow a little. Juggling the tray from the kitchen, he unlocked his door, and stepped inside.

The sight of her stole his breath away. He heard the quiet click of the door behind him, so he knew the door had shut, but he was too busy drinking in the vision in the center of his bed.

She was sitting up, with her legs tucked beneath her. She wasn't quite naked, though—she was wearing one of his white shirts. The buttons were undone, baring a strip of skin down the center of her torso, and giving him a delicious hint of her breasts.

"Are you going to just stand there, or are you going to come closer?" she asked.

He shook himself out of his reverie and nodded, setting the tray on the table. But first, he had a burning need to capture her like this. To record the moment. "Don't move." He grabbed his sketchbook off the table, then sat on the bed near her, careful not to touch her.

He knew once he touched her, he wouldn't be able to stop. He started sketching.

"Don't tense up," he said. "You're beautiful." His hand moved quickly over the page, the image of her taking shape. Desire was driving him to move faster. "Take the shirt off."

With an elegant shrug of her shoulders, the shirt slipped away. "You show that sketch to anyone and I'll hurt you."

Niko smiled. That was his Mackenna. Finally, he couldn't hold himself back any longer. He tossed the pad behind him, and reached for the tray that he'd brought from the kitchen.

"What's that?"

"A few little treats." He handed her a beer.

She smiled and tipped it back. He watched her throat work as she took a long drink. When she pulled it away, he watched her lips, envious of the bottle.

She offered it to him and he took it, placed his lips where hers had been, and took a sip of the tart drink. Then he reached out and pushed her back until she snuggled into the pillows.

"I bet I can make this taste even better." He

tipped the bottle just a little, and a few drops of amber liquid sprinkled on her thigh. Niko leaned down and licked it off her skin.

She gasped. He moved up and tipped a little more on her flat stomach. He licked that up too, taking his time.

"Are you hungry?" he murmured.

"Starving." Her tone was breathless.

He set the bottle on the bedside table and then reached for the small bowl of whipped cream on the tray. He dipped his fingers into it, touched her skin, and smeared the sweet stuff across her breasts.

"You are the most beautiful canvas I've ever used." He picked up a bowl of raspberries now, selected one fat, luscious berry, and stroked it down her skin, leaving a tantalizing smear.

He leaned down, sucking the cream off her breasts, nipping at her nipples. He lapped it all up, then started following the trail of raspberry red down her middle.

He kept rubbing the delicious food over her and licking it off, watching her writhe under his touch. Holding a berry to her lips, he watched her bite into it, her gaze hot on his. She sucked the juices off his fingers. With a growl, he lowered his head and nipped her lips. Then he moved lower, lower, between her thighs. He loved that she was clean-shaven, and he could see all of her—so pink and pretty. He put his mouth on her. As her moans filled the room, he licked and sucked and tasted her delicious flavor.

Then her hands tangled in his hair, tugging his head up.

"No," she said. "I want to come with you inside me."

The words were like gasoline to fire. With a growl, Niko sat up, and stood beside the bed. He made short work of peeling his clothes off. Her gaze went straight to his cock, which was already hard and rearing up against his belly.

A second later, he knelt between her legs, gripping her thighs and pushing them apart.

"Do you have an implant, or do I need to use a condom?" He had three that he'd traded for over the last few weeks. But three would never be enough.

She moved against the sheets. "My implant's good for a few more months."

He could have her without any barriers.

Fuck. The thought of sliding himself inside her, skin to skin, nothing between them... He was such a caveman.

He reached down and fisted his cock. Her gaze watched his hand as he pumped himself slowly. Her chest was rising and falling with every breath.

"You want this?"

She nodded.

He rubbed the swollen head of his cock against her, feeling how slick she was, how her juices lubricated him. He moved up, rubbing himself against her clit. She jerked and let out a small cry. That sound made him harder.

"How long has it been, Mackenna?"

She licked her lips. "Since before the invasion."

He liked that. That she hadn't been with anyone for a long time. "Me, too."

With a heavy gaze, she smiled at him. "But I touch myself."

It was far too easy to imagine her lying back, naked, legs splayed, with her fingers on her clit. He groaned, rubbing against her more. Then he moved just a little, the head of his cock lodging between her lips. Slowly, he pushed inside her.

She tossed her head back, moaning.

She was so tight. Niko gritted his teeth. So good.

"Stop being so slow." Her left leg shifted, coming up to clamp around his hip. "Harder. More."

His control evaporated. He slammed home, then he gripped her thighs, and started to piston inside her.

"Niko!"

The room was filled with the sounds of their moans and flesh hitting flesh. It was raw and hungry. He needed her more than he needed anything in his life.

It wasn't long before he felt the little spasms inside her. She screamed, and her body clamped down on him.

Niko shoved deep, holding himself there, and let out a roar as he spilled himself inside her.

***

Mac rested against Niko's side.

The sex had been...amazing. She snuggled into

his naked body. God, she'd never been a snuggler, but she was more than happy to stay right here.

She looked down and realized that she still had red and white stains on her from the raspberries and cream. "We made a mess."

She felt him smile against her hair. She lifted her head. He looked like some big, lazy, satisfied cat.

"I'm not sorry," he murmured.

She reached over the edge of the bed and scooped up some raspberries from the discarded bowl. She popped one in her mouth, then rubbed the other one down his chest. She leaned forward and bit him.

He growled, sitting up and scooting backward until he was resting against the headboard. He grabbed her and pulled her on top of him. She straddled his body, feeling his hard cock between her thighs.

Hmm, she liked this.

He grabbed her wrist, lifted it to his mouth, and ate the raspberry out of her hand. He sucked the juice off her fingers, and she squirmed against him. Then he pulled her hands up until her fingers curled around the headboard either side of his head. "You're in charge."

She shifted her hips, rubbing against him. "I like that."

"I can tell." He leaned forward and caught her mouth. He tasted like raspberries, his tongue sliding against hers. "What are you going to do to me, Mackenna?"

Mac rose up, positioned his cock beneath her, then sank down. She watched the pleasure cross his face. "I'm going to take you inside me."

"Do I stretch you?"

She felt every inch of him slide inside her. "Yes."

Then there was no room for talking. She moved her hips, finding her rhythm, and rode him. Soon, she was slamming down on him, desperate for the relief she felt shimmering just out of reach.

"Mackenna." He bumped his hips up to meet her, his hands digging into her hips.

Then she felt one hand slide down between their bodies, his thumb rubbing across her swollen clit.

She came, her back arching. She threw her head back, trying to stifle her screams. He grabbed her hips, pulled her down, and came a second later, his big body shuddering.

Mac slumped forward, her head resting on his shoulder. She stayed there, glued to him by the light sheen of perspiration on them. He stroked a hand down her back, tracing her spine.

"I'm so very glad you came to the Enclave," he said.

She turned her head and kissed his ear. "Me, too. Even if you are corrupting me and ruining my reputation."

His fingers gripped her chin and urged her head up. "Here, in this room, you don't need the armor, Mackenna. It's just you and me. All I need is for you to be yourself."

She blew out a breath. "The tough part *is* me, Niko."

"Bullshit. Sure, it's one aspect, but it doesn't define you."

"It's been bred into me."

He touched her cheek. "By your father."

She wasn't sure how she felt talking about her dad right now. "He was a good man. Decent and hardworking. But he had no idea what to do with three kids, let alone a daughter."

"He should have just let you be yourself."

"It wasn't bad. I loved hunting, fishing, shooting. And I loved the traveling."

"But?"

She snuggled in deeper, listening to his heartbeat. "Okay. Maybe I wished for a home sometimes. A place where I could cook, collect a few pretty things. We moved around so much, we just couldn't take too much with us. I had this doll once..." She pulled a face. "I, ah, borrowed it from the local store. He made me pay for it, and then leave it behind when we left for his next job." She deepened her voice. "*Don't get attached, Mac.*"

Niko's arm tightened on her. "I don't mind if you get attached to me."

God, and she would. This man could be an addiction she might never recover from.

"I won't be a pretty ornament hanging off your arm, Niko. The Enclave leader's pretty piece."

He snorted out a laugh. "God, perish the thought. I'm not a damn politician. Just be you. That's all I want."

Mac felt a shot of heat in her belly.

Then a big hand slid down and cupped her

breast, stroking her nipple. She pressed into his touch.

"You'll have to get used to me spoiling you, though. There are enough tough, hard circumstances in our new world. I want to give you nice things. I want to feed your sweet tooth and make you come multiple times a day."

Mac laughed. "Giving me daily orgasms is spoiling me?"

He stroked her jaw. "I want you to collect those pretty things, Mackenna. With me. Now how about a shower?"

***

With steam rising around him, Niko slapped his palms against the tile to hold himself upright. He fought back a strangled moan. Mac was on her knees between his legs, sucking his cock down her throat.

The sensations were roaring through him, strong and steady. Hell, her mouth...it was so damn good.

He felt his orgasm threatening, coiling low. He leaned down, slipped his hands under her arms, and pulled her up.

"I wasn't finished," she complained.

Niko couldn't form the words to reply—desire was riding him too hard. He spun her, palmed her tight butt, and slid inside her.

Their cries echoed off the walls, the wet slap of flesh inflaming him more. He thrust into her again and again.

A second later, they both groaned as they came.

"I can't walk," she said.

With a flick of his wrist, Niko turned off the water. He scooped her up into his arms. "We've been fucking all day, so it's time to refuel. Time to head down to the dining room for a meal." He needed some food or he'd pass out.

She groaned. "Why can't we stay here?"

Because his inner caveman wanted to show her off. Wanted to make his claim public.

"Come on, Carides." He set her down and gave her a light slap on the butt. "I expected more stamina than this."

She glared daggers at him, then grabbed her clothes off the floor and started to dress.

They held hands as they walked toward the dining room. He was surprised she let him, but as they got closer and could hear the murmur of voices, she tried to pull her hand away.

"No." He held on tightly.

"I know what you're doing," she muttered.

"Holding the hand of my woman? Enjoying her touch?"

"Beating your chest."

"Don't you want the women to know I'm off-limits?"

She leaned in close. "I shouldn't need to advertise the fact we're sleeping together for them to keep their hands off you. Trusting you should be enough."

Niko grinned at her. She trusted him. Damn, a

gift like Mackenna Carides' trust seemed better than a roomful of treasure. "You *can* trust me."

She gave him a nod, then her eyes narrowed. "But be warned. If I catch you touching someone else—" she lowered her voice "—I'll kill you."

He shook his head. "You are so damn sexy."

She was laughing when he tugged her inside the dining room. He noted a few curious looks, and then he spotted a table at the back. Squad Nine was sitting with Hell Squad.

"Hallelujah," Cam cried out as they made their way over. "Mac finally got laid."

Mac scowled at her friend. "A bit louder, Cam. I don't think they heard you in Outer Mongolia."

Cam rubbed her hands together. "That just leaves Taylor and Theron for me to sort out."

"What about me?" Sienna asked.

"Sweet Sienna, you just bat those lashes of yours and flash those pretty curves, and you have men falling all over your feet."

The brunette pouted. "But they never stick around. I intimidate them or something. And, well, they're all kind of boring. They're vanilla gelato, and I'm a chocolate-with-sprinkles-on-top kind of girl."

Marcus nodded his head toward some spare chairs. "Take a seat. If you hang around with these ladies long enough, you'll get used to this."

From nearby, Reed Mackinnon rolled his eyes. "No you don't." His fiancé, Natalya smiled from beside him.

As Niko and Mac sat, he saw Elle smiling at them.

"Hi," she said. "I heard about the hairy mission."

Niko felt Mackenna's hand flex on his. "Thanks, Elle," he said. "Everyone's okay. Any update on the drone parts we recovered?"

Elle shook her head. "Noah thinks he might get some information off it, but he is still working on it."

"Dev and Santha's intel guys are going over the photos," Marcus added. "They're researching everything we have on birds of prey—eagles, hawks. Trying to do up a profile on its behavior."

Plates of food were delivered a moment later, but Niko was lost in thought. They needed more than this. They needed to find the damn drone killer and finish it before it took down more of their drones.

Or worse. He looked down at the woman by his side. Before the damn thing got someone killed.

Chapter Eleven

Mac liked the table in the conference room off the Command Center. It was a large, black, glossy affair, and if the situation wasn't so serious, it would give her some naughty little fantasies.

But right now, it was covered in maps, papers, and sketches. The screens on the wall displayed electronic maps with the downed drone locations marked on them, and that nest they'd investigated at the tanks at the airport.

Niko stood with his hands pressed to the table. He had his sleeves rolled up, and her gaze kept moving to his muscular forearms. They made her think of what the two of them had done all day yesterday and all night. She felt a flush of heat in her cheeks.

For the first time, she admitted to herself that she was falling for him.

Her sexy Russian artist was seducing her. Making her believe that she could have it all—her job, her man, indulge in the little things she enjoyed...and love. Most of all, he made her believe in love.

At that moment he looked up and gave her a

smile. But it was strained. He was stressed about finding the drone killer. She turned her head, and stared at the electronic sketch on the screen. They'd all pooled their impressions of the animal. It looked like a hawk, but with black, leathery scales. It had the sleek body of a bird of prey, and Roth had said he'd seen eerie green eyes.

"Maybe the aliens keep it locked away?" she suggested. "Caged somewhere."

Niko's jaws tightened. "Maybe they're making more of them."

There was a gasp from the doorway.

Mac turned and spotted the slim figure, but not before she saw Niko stiffen a little.

Selena was a shock to the system, at first. It was strange to have an alien in the heart of their base.

"Hi, Selena," Mac said.

"Mac." The alien woman had a soft, melodic voice.

Her skin was incredibly pale, and her long hair was white. No, that wasn't quite right. It was kind of shiny and pearlescent. She had large, green eyes in a delicate face. She'd been rescued from alien captivity along with Claudia Frost. Her species was an enemy of the Gizzida.

But Mac knew that many Enclave members were still unsettled by her. She'd been sticking to herself and laying low since they'd arrived.

Mac turned her chair. "How are you doing?"

The woman gave a tiny shrug. "Fine. Thank you." Sadness was like a shroud around her.

Mac couldn't imagine what it felt like to be stuck

on a planet, far from those you loved, with no way home.

A frown marred Selena's face. "But I wanted to ask why you have a picture of a gyr?"

Mac straightened. "A what?"

Selena walked closer and pointed at the image on the screen. "It looks a bit different...its skin isn't right. But this is a bird from my planet, Florum."

Mac's heart skipped a beat. She shared a look with Niko.

He pulled out a chair and gestured. "Please take a seat, Selena. Tell us more."

"The eyes give it away." She waved at her own face and her overlarge green eyes. "We all have green eyes. It fascinates me to see the variety of eye colors in humans."

"So this bird looks like a gyr from your world?" Mac repeated. "But it also looks different?"

She nodded. "The black scaled exterior is different. On Florum, they are usually white. They are excellent hunters and ambush prey from the clouds."

Niko started scribbling down notes.

Selena's face turned sad. "The Gizzida took it, didn't they? They twisted the gyr."

Mac blew out a breath. "It looks that way. They've bred this thing to hunt our drones."

Selena shifted in her chair. "The gyr are a very rare bird. The Gizzida couldn't have more than one."

"But surely they could genetically engineer more?" Niko said.

"No." Selena pushed her hair back. "They can alter a living being, but they can't create one from nothing."

Sitting back in her chair, Mac considered Selena's words. They all knew why the Gizzida had come to Earth—for the resources and the main resource was human bodies for their genesis tanks. To create more raptor soldiers.

"It's highly doubtful they have more," Selena continued. "The gyr only breed once every five of your Earth years."

"Well, that's a bit of good luck then." Niko shoved his hands in his pockets. "Anything else you think might be relevant to us catching this thing?"

"They like to live near the water."

Mac nodded. "We found its nest." She tapped the keyboard and the image of the tanks and the gyr nest appeared. "It's right near the harbor and the alien ship."

Selena frowned and leaned forward. "That's not its nest."

"What?" Mac frowned. "It looks like a nest."

"The gyr have...hunting outposts." She moved a hand like she was searching for the right word. "Way stations. They store things there, but it isn't where they sleep or spend the majority of their time. Its main nest would be on top of the water, surrounded by water."

"Really?" Mac looked at Niko. "We need to get the intel team running some searches. Find any possible offshore locations that might work."

"We don't have drones offshore. Or recent maps

of the area," Niko said in a dark tone.

"We'll find it," Mac said.

"Gyr are very skilled hunters," Selena said. "Their sense of smell is beyond anything we have ever encountered on Florum. My guess is this creature is smelling your drones."

An alarm blared. Selena jumped and Mac jolted, ready to leap to her feet. She had to remind herself that she wasn't on duty today. "Thanks, Selena."

Niko and Mac rushed into the main Command Center area.

Elle was at a comp with a headset on. "Head northwest of the Enclave, Marcus. Twenty kilometers."

"Got it, Elle." Marcus' voice came across the speakers.

On the screen, Mac saw Hell Squad sitting in a Hawk. "What's going on?"

"Survivors coming in." Elle's pretty face hardened. "Aliens are in pursuit."

"Are we sure they aren't hybrids this time?" Niko put his hands on his hips, watching the screen.

"Lia has a drone going in close now to confirm," Elle replied.

They all watched, tense and apprehensive, as Lia's drone zoomed in closer to the frightened survivors. God, this was so much worse than being in the field. There was no way she could be a comms officer.

These survivors were clearly making a run toward the Enclave. In the back of an open truck,

Mac saw a group of people with gaunt, frightened faces and threadbare clothes. Her gut cramped. A lot of them were kids.

A chair scraped loudly against the floor, and there was a strangled cry. A woman at one of the comp stations was standing and swaying on her feet. Her face was white.

"That's...that's my husband." Tears welled in her eyes. "In the red shirt. That's Jacob. He wasn't selected for the Enclave. He made me come with our daughter." She pressed a fist to her mouth. "I thought he was dead."

Jesus. Mac watched as Hell Squad's Hawk raced closer to the truck. And the aliens' big, rugged, black vehicle did too.

Niko stared up at the screens. "Let's bring them home."

***

Niko's pulse was drumming. It felt like a ticking clock. He watched as the ugly, squat vehicle moved closer to the survivors' truck.

Then the raptor vehicle opened fire.

Shit. Niko tapped his fingers on the desk in front of him. He saw the truck swerving madly to avoid the raptor poison. In the back, adults covered the children with their bodies. One survivor toppled out of the truck bed with a bloodcurdling scream.

Chyort! How long until Hell Squad reached them?

The muscles in Niko's neck and shoulders felt

stretched to their breaking point. He felt the terror of the woman, Anne, whose husband was in the truck. She was wringing her hands and quietly murmuring prayers.

"Bugs!" Elle cried out. "Marcus, watch out, you have alien bugs in the vicinity."

Niko searched the screen and then he spotted them. The alien bugs looked like mutant dragonflies. They had long, elongated bodies, and two sets of transparent wings. Their heads had large, multifaceted eyes and their mouths had serrated mandibles on either side.

He watched in horror as one of the bugs reached the back of the truck and snapped at the humans. With a cry, a woman was wrenched out of the truck.

He heard Anne gasp. Her husband was shielding a group of children.

President Howell had died like this—taken by an alien bug. The bastard deserved it. Niko couldn't believe the man had separated couples and families. All so he could pick the best of the best. Scientists, artists, the most intelligent...Howell had planned his own little utopia with himself at the helm.

"Anne, maybe you want to wait outside," Niko suggested.

"No." The woman grabbed his arm, her fingernails digging into his skin. "Bring him home. *Please*. Bring them home safely, Nikolai."

He patted her arm. "We will." Niko hoped it wasn't a lie.

Finally, he saw the quadcopter appear, dropping its illusion. Hell Squad had arrived.

Laser fire joined the fray. The alien vehicle swerved to avoid it.

Mackenna moved up beside Niko and slipped her hand into his. They watched as the fight turned chaotic. Hell Squad fought hard and fast, and Elle continued to murmur information to her team. The alien vehicle skidded to a halt, raptors pouring out.

"Marcus, you have seven raptors exiting the vehicle," Elle said. "Standard raptor weapons."

Suddenly, a black shadow darted in front of the drone. A loud screech echoed from the speakers.

"Drone killer," Lia said from another comp station. "I repeat, the drone killer is in the area." She looked back at Niko. "Do you want me to pull the drones back? Or do we keep them there?"

Before he had the chance to respond, the drone shook. Something had impacted it. Hard. It fell from the sky in a dizzying spiral.

Lia cursed, fighting to regain control. A second later, the drone crashed into the ground and the screen went black.

Shit. But they still had another in the air.

"I'm taking over the final drone," Lia said. Then she barked orders to her drone operators through her headset.

Niko watched as Lia flew the drone in a mad dance through the sky to avoid the drone killer chasing it. Lia was using some pretty fancy flying to stay out of the bird's reach. But it also meant this footage was shaky, blurry, and not aimed where they needed it.

"Keep going, Lia," Elle said. "That drone is relaying back the audio as well. We can't lose it."

Niko got a glimpse of Hell Squad reaching the truck. He saw kids being handed down to Marcus. The rest of Hell Squad was engaging the approaching aliens.

Then the image was gone, and all he saw was blue sky and cloud. There was the odd glimpse of the drone killer's sleek, black body.

"I can't keep this up." Lia's voice was strained.

Dammit. Niko drummed his fingers on the desk, felt Mac squeeze his other hand. Did he risk keeping the drone out there, or did he cut off contact with Hell Squad to save it? Without the drone, they couldn't call for backup, and had no intel from Elle.

"The damn drone killer is closing in," Lia cried. "We can't afford to lose another drone!"

Niko stared at the wild footage shaking across the screen. It wasn't helping them. "Pull the drone back."

"No." Anne cried. "What about the survivors?"

"Hell Squad will bring them home. Lia, move the drone back to a safe distance but try to stay in range to keep the audio. Elle, tell Marcus we might lose contact."

The drone retreated, whizzing away from the combat area. The audio was still loud and clear.

"Cruz, get the kids on the Hawk." Marcus' voice was a loud roar. "Everyone else. Run! Get to that quadcopter." There was the sound of laser fire and raptor weapons. It sounded like it was right on top of them.

God, it was horrible to listen to. Niko dragged in a breath.

And then he heard Cruz cursing in Spanish. "They lobbed some sort of grenade. Watch out!"

Now there was screaming.

"Fuck. People are hit. I repeat people are hit," Cruz said.

Niko turned to look at Elle. "Backup?"

"I've already activated Squad Three. They'll be there in a few minutes." Elle's voice was shaky but calm.

"Shit!" Cruz again. "Marcus is hit. I repeat Marcus is down."

At the comp, Elle went pale. She gripped her keyboard. "Cruz—"

"I've got him, Ellie. He's paralyzed by the raptor poison, but he's alive."

But Niko knew that raptor poison burned and ate through flesh. Beside him, Anne was sobbing, and gulping in shallow breaths.

Niko looked at Mackenna. Her face was grim, but she leaned into him. Giving him her support.

"Arriving at the scene." Tane Rahia's cool voice came across the line.

"Tane, this is Lia. Any sign of the drone killer?"

A pause.

"Nothing."

"Screw this." Lia spun. "I'm taking the drone back in."

"Do it," Niko said.

A minute later, the screens flickered back to life. One displayed the drone feed, and the other the video from Tane's helmet camera.

The scene was filled with carnage.

Hell Squad was fighting, giving cover to the survivors, who were running for the Hawk. Some were huddled in a frightened group near their truck. Niko's stomach dropped away. There were lots of bodies on the ground. Too many.

And one was a man, sprawled facedown and wearing a red shirt.

Niko heard a keening cry beside him. He spun and caught Anne as her legs gave out.

Then she straightened and shoved against him. "You were supposed to save him!" She hammered at Niko's chest. "He'd survived all this time..." Tears were falling down her face. "This is like losing him all over again." She broke down, sobbing.

Niko pulled her close, helpless to soothe her suffering. He heard another noise and looked up.

Anne's young daughter was standing in the doorway, staring at the screen with a pale face. "Daddy?"

For a second, Niko was in another time and place. Watching another young girl staring at her father's dead body.

Another technician stood and pried Anne away from Niko. With an arm wrapped around the sobbing woman, the other female technician led Anne and her daughter away.

Back on the screen, Gabe Jackson was carrying

Marcus onto the Hawk. Soon, Hell Squad and the remaining survivors were aboard, and the Hawk lifted off.

Squad Three remained on the ground, busy mowing through the few remaining aliens.

Niko flexed his hands and closed his eyes.

Mackenna's firm touch was on his arm. "It's not your fault, Niko."

So why did it feel like it was?

He turned around and stormed out.

Chapter Twelve

Mac found Niko in his apartment. The lights were on low and there was a half empty bottle of vodka beside him.

She'd expected him to be splattering paint across canvas, but he was sitting at a small table. His hands were moving in slow, methodical movements, and were covered in something gray. Clay, she realized. He was sculpting.

He was shirtless, his jeans riding low on his hips. His face was set like stone and a brooding presence filled the air.

"Niko."

"I'm not good company right now, Mackenna."

"They made it back. Marcus and the others are in the infirmary."

A muscle ticked in Niko's jaw. "Not all of them. Not Anne's husband."

Mac approached, aching for him. "I think—"

"They're dead. I should've left the drone there. I should have sent more squads in the first place. I should've found the drone killer by now." He slammed his hand down on the table, making his art supplies rattle. "I should've done *something*."

Mac realized she'd seen more death and

suffering at Blue Mountain Base. They'd been going out to fight the aliens every day, they'd been under attack, they'd suffered casualties. Maybe she'd become a little numb to the losses.

But despite his assassin background, Niko and the people of the Enclave had been more insulated since the invasion. She loved the fact that he felt so deeply, but she didn't want him to suffer, to take on a guilt that wasn't his.

"Niko, we're in the middle of a war. There will be casualties." She felt a pain in her heart. "There'll be more before this is over."

He looked up at her, his eyes stormy. "My work for Russian Intelligence...it was all about death." He looked down at his hands. "At first, I was proud. I was working for my country, doing a difficult job...but I never once questioned my orders."

His accent had thickened, and Mackenna forced herself to stay still and listen.

"They sent me to kill a man, a traitor, just outside Moscow." Now Niko looked at the wall, lost in his painful memories. "I killed him. And then realized his small daughter was watching. She looked at me like I was a monster and it made me realize that I was. After that, I found out that the man wasn't a traitor." Niko blew out a breath. "He was just a citizen who disagreed with the government. They made me into a murderer." Then he shook his head angrily. "No, that isn't right. No one else is to blame for what I did except myself."

"What did you do after that?"

"I left. Disappeared. I did what I did best, and

used my considerable skills to vanish."

She knew he would have been very good at it. And she knew his former bosses would've tried to hunt him down.

"I was hiding among the artist community in New York when I picked up my first paintbrush. And then I started carving this beautiful piece of mahogany..." He looked up at her. "For once, I was creating and making something beautiful, instead of killing and destroying."

Mac felt a desperate need to touch him. She reached out and gently touched his shoulder. "Niko, you've made something here at the Enclave. A home, a haven, a sanctuary. Without your leadership, most of these people wouldn't have made it."

Emotion spasmed over his face. "I should have done more to save those people today. If I hadn't been caught up, so distracted by..."

When his words drifted away, Mac raised a brow. She absorbed the pain that pierced her chest. "Go on. Distracted by fucking me? By me sucking your cock in the shower? By—"

"Stop it," he bit off.

"You started it, damn you. You know what, Niko? Those deaths today—Anne's husband—it isn't about you. You should be focused on fighting back, not blaming yourself and wallowing in it."

He reached out and yanked her into his lap. She stayed stiff in his arms.

"I'm sorry," he murmured. He pressed his face against her neck. "I'm sorry."

She tried to stay hard, but she couldn't. She sagged against him, holding on tight. God, he was melting something inside her, and for once, she didn't care. For him, she could have a soft spot.

He reached up, his hand circling her throat and smearing clay on her skin. "I don't regret a single second with you, Mackenna. You make it bearable. You make it all worthwhile." He leaned forward and kissed her.

This kiss was slow, gentle, and it felt different from everything they'd shared before. Mac felt butterflies in her stomach.

"It's okay, Niko. I'm here when you need me. But don't think I won't kick your ass when you need it."

His smile was faint, but it was there. "We should go and check on the injured. On Marcus."

She nodded and slipped off his lap. She watched as he grabbed his shirt, pulled it on, and took a second to wash his hands.

He held her hand in a death grip as they walked down to the infirmary.

And once again, Mac found herself in that plush waiting room that she was beginning to hate. All of Squad Nine, and Hell Squad, and their partners were there—worried and waiting. Cruz was holding a shaken Elle in his arms.

"Any news?" Niko asked.

Cruz shook his head.

Elle turned teary eyes their way. "Marcus never gets hurt. He's so big, so strong, so…"

Seemingly indestructible. But Mac knew the risks they took every time they went out there. Any of them could get hurt.

Niko's hand tightened on hers and she knew he was thinking the same thing.

When Niko wandered over to talk with Roth and Cruz, Cam came over to Mac. "You have clay on you." She waved at the neck of Mac's shirt.

Damn. Mac had forgotten about it. She glanced down at herself. Well, there wasn't much she could do about it.

Cam smiled. "It's the perfect imprint of big, strong fingers. I'm happy for you, babe."

"Thanks, Cam."

"Wish I could find a hunk of sexy who looks at me like he looks at you."

"Cam, you have it. You're so busy beating him up because you're afraid."

"Afraid?" Cam made a hissing sound. "You're talking about *Hemi*?" She shook her head. "Screw that. I don't need that annoying, scruffy Neanderthal—"

"You ever hear that one about protesting too much?"

Cam's mouth snapped shut and she crossed her arms over her chest. "Shut up."

The infirmary door opened, and everyone in the waiting room glanced up. Mac expected to see Doc Emerson.

Instead, it was a shirtless, shoeless Marcus Steele in the doorway. His scarred face was a little pale and he had a white bandage on his shoulder, but other than that, he looked his usual tough self.

"Marcus." Elle rushed forward.

He pulled her in tight against him. And the look that crossed his face... Mac swallowed the lump in her throat. She felt like she was witnessing something private and intimate.

"Marcus!" Doc Emerson's annoyed voice. "I said you couldn't get out of bed yet!" The doctor squeezed around the Hell Squad soldier. "You are so stubborn." Then, Emerson looked at Elle, and a reluctant smile curved her lips. "He's wanted to see you from the moment he woke up." She looked back at her patient with a scowl. "He was all grumpy and grouchy. Alpha males make the *worst* patients."

"He's okay?" Elle asked, clinging to her fiancé.

"Fine. Although his nanomeds aren't quite finished yet. Hence the staying. In. Bed. Thing."

"I'm not staying," Marcus said firmly.

"You are," the doctor replied darkly.

Elle moved her hand over Marcus' chest. "Can I stay with him?"

"Sure."

Marcus made a few grumbling sounds, but he let Elle lead him back into the infirmary.

Mac sighed. That was what love looked like. Neither Marcus nor Elle were soft. Instead, they'd learned to bend a little—but that made them stronger, not weaker.

When Niko returned to her, Mac let herself lean into his side.

***

Niko sat at the table in his room, carefully mixing the lotion in the pretty glass jar he'd bartered a little painting for. Beside him was a bowl of smooshed raspberries, and another filled with plain lotion he'd gotten from one of the Enclave ladies who made the best lotions, moisturizers, and toiletries in the place.

He wanted something special for Mackenna. Something to feed that little love of nice things. He had a few discarded batches of virulent pink sitting beside him. He'd tried mixing the raspberries in, but he'd put too much, and the early batches were far too strong. The bright pink creams stained everything—skin, clothes, hands.

In this next batch, he put just the tiniest bit of raspberry, then mixed in the other ingredients. He stirred it and leaned down to sniff it. *Perfect.* Just a hint of sweet scent. He imagined rubbing it on her belly, her thighs, her breasts. He imagined sliding his hands between her legs—

"Hey?"

Her voice made him jolt.

She stepped in front of him, eyeing him with a narrowed gaze. "What are you doing?"

He cleared his throat and held out the jar. "I was making a present for you."

"Really?" Her face lightened and she took the jar and held it up. "But you were thinking about sex. You get this look."

He grinned at her. "I was thinking about what I'd do with this."

She smelled the lotion and a sweet, very un-Mac

look crossed her face. "Raspberries. It's lovely." She tilted her head. "So where would you rub it?"

"All over you."

She leaned down and kissed him. In a flash, desire ignited in his gut. How the hell could she take him from sweet happiness to raging lust in just seconds? "Damn, Mackenna, one kiss from you, and you have me as hard as steel."

She reached down and boldly stroked him through his trousers. "I was coming to get you. We have a meeting about the drone killer in ten minutes."

He pulled her closer. "I can work with ten minutes." He started unbuttoning her trousers.

"But we need four minutes to walk to the Command Center, so that only leaves you six," she said, voice breathless.

Niko delved his hand between her legs. She was already wet for him. "I like a challenge." Quickly, he turned her away from him, palming her sweet ass. He reached down and freed his cock.

Without warning her, he pulled her down, lodging his cock deep inside her with a groan. She made a strangled sound and he bumped his hips up against her. He kept his thrusts short, hard, and fast. He moved his hands between her legs, arrowing in on that slick little nub.

"Yes, Niko!"

He felt his release roaring closer and kept working her clit. He wanted her to come first. A second after she cried out his name, Niko unloaded his release inside her.

They were five minutes late to the meeting. From Cam's wide grin, Niko guessed no one was fooled as to why they were late.

But once he saw the screens, he felt the happiness and ease from their quickie fade away.

The screen showed the interior of a Hawk. It was flying out across the ocean below. He could just see a set of hands at the Hawk controls and one slim shoulder on the other side of the cockpit.

Holmes stepped forward. "I authorized a mission to take a drone into the suspected drone killer area. The plan is to run the drone from the Hawk. Any sign of trouble, they'll bring the drone in."

"Erickson's at the controls?" Niko asked.

Elle turned from her comp screen. "Yes. Lia is also aboard."

"How far from Sydney Airport?"

"Several kilometers offshore. Their illusion system is up and Finn is the best we have at evading alien detection."

Everyone watched as the Hawk sped above the waves. Tension pulsed in the room.

"You're too low, Erickson." Lia's tart voice.

"I'm the pilot here. No backseat pilots allowed."

Lia sniffed. "I can fly too, you know."

There was a snort. "Not like me."

"Arrogant flight jockey."

Elle spoke into her headset, her voice amused. "We can hear you, guys. Everyone in the Command Center can hear you."

The bickering fell quiet.

"There's something ahead," Finn said, his voice now serious.

Niko saw Lia's shoulder as she leaned forward. "What *is* that?"

The image of a long, black shape atop the water appeared on the screen.

"Releasing the drone," Lia said.

A second later, Niko saw the small drone whizz past the cockpit of the Hawk and disappear as its illusion system flicked on.

Its camera feed filled another screen. At first, there was only water, then the hulking black shape in the distance came into view.

"It looks like a...battleship, or an aircraft carrier," someone said.

"An alien battleship." A rock settled in Niko's gut. The black ship loomed ahead, with long, antenna-like protrusions, and a large, bulky bridge at the back.

He could see raptors walking about on the deck. Strange equipment dotted the deck of the ship, pulsing red.

"My God." It was Lia's shocked voice.

Niko frowned, and as the drone adjusted course, he saw what she'd spotted.

Right on the bow of the ship was a huge nest. Many times larger than the one from the tanks.

And sitting on top of it was the drone killer.

It was the best view they'd had of the bird. It looked far more monstrous than in their sketches. It had a sleek body, but its stocky power was obvious.

It lifted its head. And looked directly at the camera. At the drone.

With a single flap of wings, it took off.

"Goddammit," Lia said.

The drone spun away and they lost their view of the ship. Niko watched as the drone sped up, zooming away from its pursuer.

There was an earsplitting shriek. The drone killer was gaining.

"It's coming." Finn's tense voice.

"Open the side door," Lia said. "I'm going to do a hot landing inside the Hawk."

Finn's body blocked the camera's view, as he went into the back of the quadcopter to open the side door. Then he was back in the cockpit, sitting beside Lia.

"Come on," she murmured, fully focused on the drone controls.

"You can do this, Lia," Finn said quietly.

Niko's gut was tight. How close was the drone killer? He silently urged the little drone to move faster. Then the drone feed showed it was nearing the Hawk.

The bird was in hot pursuit.

"Almost there," Lia said. "Get ready."

Finn moved into the back again. There was a *thunk* from nearby.

"Drone's inside the Hawk!" Finn cried out. "I've got it."

Then there was another clang as something else hit metal. Finn's curses filled the line.

"Oh, God." Lia pushed to her feet. "It's in the

144

Hawk!" This time, her body blocked the camera's view, as she moved into the back of the Hawk with Finn.

Everyone in the Command Center waited, holding their collective breath. They could hear Finn and Lia scuffling with something. The angry screech of a bird, more of Finn's curses.

"Watch out!" Lia shouted.

There was a loud thump.

"It's out! Get us out of here, Finn."

Seconds later, Finn and Lia pushed back into the cockpit. Finn cast one glance back at the camera, and Niko saw that the side of the Hawk pilot's face was covered in blood. Then he sank into his chair and touched the controls. The Hawk shot forward. Lia wasn't in her seat yet, and as the Hawk turned, she crashed into Finn, landing in his lap.

"Well, it wasn't what I had in mind," Finn drawled, "but feel free to stay there for the rest of the trip."

Lia cursed. "Let me up." She struggled to extricate herself.

"It'll be softer in my lap than the seat."

Lia wrenched herself away from him and pulled herself up.

"Okay, maybe not," Finn said dryly.

"Shut up, Erickson." She made it back to her seat and strapped herself in.

Back in the Command Center, everyone released shaky breaths.

"Well done, you two," Elle said. "Return to base."

Chapter Thirteen

Mac finished strapping her armor on. Around her, her squad was talking and chatting as they also completed their preparations.

They finally knew where the drone killer was.

It was time to take it down.

Together, they walked out into the corridor. They met Hell Squad leaving their locker room—all geared up and ready for the mission. The plan was that Squad Nine would take point and infiltrate the ship, and destroy the drone killer. Meanwhile, Hell Squad would wait on a second Hawk as backup.

Mac pulled in some calming breaths. She was ready. They walked into the hangar.

Ahead, Niko was waiting with Holmes. Mac's spine stiffened. Niko was wearing armor.

Memories of the last mission—his face swollen and his stomach bleeding internally—crowded into her head. "You are not coming."

He gave her a steady look. "I am. I'm still the best covert operative we have. Dev's coming, too. We need to finish this."

"And I'm coming as well."

They all turned and saw Lia stride in. She was

also wearing armor and carrying a drone in one hand.

Niko frowned at the woman. "Lia—"

"I'm bringing a drone so you won't go in blind." She glanced at Holmes. "You need me there."

Mac watched Niko and the general share a look.

Finally, Holmes nodded. "You're in. Good luck."

Hell Squad and Squad Nine split off with slaps on the back. Lia, Devlin, and Niko were with Squad Nine.

As the others boarded, Mac grabbed Niko's arm. "Don't get beaten up this time, okay?"

He smiled at her. "I'm falling in love with you, Mackenna."

What? The air caught in her lungs and her heart fluttered like crazy. She thought maybe she was having a heart attack. "You have crappy timing, Ivanov."

His smile widened. "Come on, my tough soldier. Let's go kick some alien butt."

There'd be time to talk when they got back. Together, they climbed into the Hawk.

"Ladies and gentlemen, please fasten your seatbelts." Finn came out of the cockpit with a cocky grin. Then he spotted Lia. "You get lost, Lia?"

"No." She held up her drone. "I'm on this mission."

"Wait. What?" A fierce frown crossed his face. He looked at Roth and Niko. "Who thought this was a good idea?"

"We need the drone, Finn," Roth said. "And Lia can hold her own."

Lia's expression turned stubborn. "Thank you, Roth." She speared Finn with her gaze. "Plus, this damn drone killer has been taking down my drones. Now I'm taking *it* down."

Finn's jaw worked as he stared at the woman for a long moment. "Fine. Strap in." He spun and stormed back into the cockpit, with Lia following him.

Cam leaned over. "I give it two weeks before they're banging each other's brains out."

"A month," Taylor piped up from her seat.

"I think they'll drag this bickering thing out." Sienna gave a little shiver. "Such anticipation. So sexy. Two months."

"What makes you think they haven't already?" Dev asked.

Cam's eyes narrowed. "You know something we don't?"

Dev gave an elegant shrug. "A spy never tells."

"One week." Theron's voice was a deep rumble.

Everyone stared at him.

"Not you, too," Roth said with a groan.

Mac shook her head at the teasing. When Niko traced his hand over her arm, she looked at him.

"I love seeing you like this. Ready to take on the world." He lowered his voice to a murmur. "I like you naked, too."

"We get in, destroy the drone killer, and get out." She touched his face. "No heroic sacrifices this time, Ivanov. Promise?"

"Promise."

"And if you keep that promise, I'll show you my

appreciation later."

He touched his tongue to his teeth. "You're on."

As the Hawk lifted off and headed out toward the coast, it was filled with quiet murmurs, jokes, and teasing. The familiar banter of a well-oiled team heading out to face danger together. Mac loved her squad. They were her family, her friends, her everything. She saw Cam wink at her, and Sienna give her a thumbs-up. For the first time, Mac realized that they accepted her as she was. All of her.

And so did Niko.

She straightened. She suddenly wanted this mission over. For the first time in a long time, she didn't want to think about her job, or the aliens, or fighting.

She just wanted to enjoy her man.

It wasn't long before she saw the long, dark shadow of the raptor battleship ahead. She checked her carbine and then looked up at Niko.

"Let's do this."

***

Niko stared out of the Hawk and down at the ugly ship below. It was like a big black stain on the beautiful ocean.

He scanned the sky around them. He knew the second Hawk carrying Hell Squad was out there somewhere.

"Drone out," Lia said.

"Okay, everyone listen up." Roth stood, claiming

their attention. "Cam, Taylor, Sienna, and Theron, you're staying onboard. I want aerial cover from you *if* we need it. Be ready. If we need you, I'll call you."

The squad members nodded.

Roth looked at Niko, Mac, and Dev. "Ready?"

"Ready," Mac answered.

They clipped onto zip lines and tossed them over the side. It was a quick rappel down, and soon their boots hit the deck of the alien battleship.

The thing was *huge*.

Instantly, they brought their carbines up and moved quickly and quietly into cover.

Roth gestured, and they started moving toward the bow of the ship.

"Raptors coming up the stairs on the port side," Lia said in their earpieces.

Each of them had attached special silencers to their carbines. It wouldn't make the weapon entirely silent, but it did significantly muffle the sound. They moved into position near the doorway of the stairs. When the raptors stepped out on deck, they took them down quickly.

Niko helped Roth drag the bodies out of the way, so they were hidden behind some equipment.

Niko looked ahead, studying the route between them and the nest at the front of the ship. "This way." He led them into a maze of equipment. Everything hummed quietly, red lights glowing. In places, he saw organic-looking scales and skin covering bizarre devices. It was strange and unnerving. He looked back and saw the red lights blinking over Mac's face.

"Devlin—"

"Already a step ahead of you." Dev held up his camera and started snapping shots of the alien equipment before they started moving again.

They were getting closer to the front of the ship.

"More raptors—" Lia's frantic voice. "Hell, and I've just spotted the drone killer. It's in the air!"

They turned a corner, and the raptors were right there. The aliens gave startled grunts, and lifted their weapons.

Instantly, Niko and the others sprung into action. It was like they'd been working as a team for years.

Mac took out a raptor at point-blank range. Roth slammed one alien into the side of some raptor equipment. They swung around, wrestling each other. Niko brought his weapon up, taking a shot. His raptor fell with a gurgle. Beside him, Dev was fighting with a graceful edge, sliding down and knocking the feet out from a raptor before taking him out.

And Mac...she was tough. Fierce. His.

Soon, the raptors were all down. Niko and his team were splattered with blood, but alive and unharmed.

Then he looked up and saw the fierce shape of the drone killer, darting quickly through the sky after Lia's invisible drone.

Chyort! "Lia! Bring the drone back in. We want the drone killer down here and we can't risk losing another drone."

"Roger that. But you'll have no intel."

"Understood."

The four of them crept forward. It wasn't much farther. Niko could see a glimpse of the nest ahead.

"Roth? Niko?" It was Lia again. "The drone's coming in, but I have to warn you, I picked up a large group of raptors. They're between you and the nest. They are cutting you off."

Niko stumbled to a halt, the others doing the same.

Goddammit!

***

Shit. Mac looked around, but she knew they were short on options. She saw Roth doing the same.

Suddenly, Niko wrenched open a door. "Inside."

"What?" she exclaimed. He wanted them to go down in the ship?

"We'll head down and then come back up on the other side."

"This is crazy, Niko. We have no idea what we'll meet down there."

He raised a brow. "You have a better idea?"

No. She didn't.

Roth nodded. "Let's move."

They headed down the stairs, careful not to make any sound. The interior of the alien ship glowed with an eerie red light, and echoed with an incessant hum. They moved carefully down a long hallway. It was flanked by doorways made of a glowing amber glass. Mac could hear voices through the doors—grunts, screeches and screams.

Then, she heard the thump of boots on the floor ahead of them. *Damn.* She froze and signaled the others.

"In here." Niko nodded toward an open doorway and stepped inside.

The room was filled with pipes and organic-looking cables traveling up to the ceiling. The cables were pulsing. The team moved through, sometimes having to turn sideways to squeeze into narrow gaps. Mac was careful not to touch anything, but she did bump into a cable. A sticky, clear goo clung to her armor and she grimaced. It looked like snot.

"Raptors," Devlin murmured urgently. "Hide."

Heart hammering, Mac squeezed in between two bits of equipment. Niko was close by, looking cool and calm. She wondered how many times he'd had to hide, with his enemies bearing down on him.

They all stood there, silent, waiting for the raptors to pass. Finally, the aliens moved on.

Mac blew out a breath and climbed out of her hiding spot. She could tell Niko was good at this. It was easy to see how he'd become one of the most infamous assassins in Russian Intelligence.

But she'd also seen him talking to Enclave members, laughing with children, and creating his beautiful artwork. He was good at those things, too.

They quietly moved out of the room and up a set of stairs. Soon, they came out a door and were back out on the deck, glorious sunshine beaming down on them.

And just ahead, was the nest.

But it was empty. No drone killer.

Roth signaled and they moved cautiously toward the nest. As they got close, Mac heard strange noises coming from inside it. *What the hell?*

She touched the side of the nest, going up on her toes to look over the side—

Suddenly, something dived out of the air with a screech. She felt the sharp sting of claws at her face, the drone killer in front of her, flapping its wings and attacking.

Mac fell to the deck, trying to evade those wicked claws.

"Mackenna!"

Laser fire exploded nearby, then she heard the bird screech again and take off with a flap of wings.

"Target it!" Niko called out.

Mac rolled. She saw the men all firing upward.

But movement behind them caught her attention. Raptors were pouring out of the door they'd used as an exit. She raised her carbine and opened fire.

The drone killer circled around and came back down, landing right near Mac. Its bright-green eyes bored into her.

As Niko and the others spun and started firing at the raptors, Mac lifted her weapon and aimed it at the bird.

Then, she hesitated, just for a second. *Damn.* It was almost beautiful, regal...

She couldn't afford for it to live, but she was well aware that it was a victim, too.

"More raptors," Roth yelled.

Mac could hear the thundering of boots on metal. Projectiles whizzed past her head and she ducked.

"Fuck. There are too many," Niko shouted. "Have the rest of your squad and Hell Squad move in. The drone killer is the priority. Take it down."

Mac saw Roth waving a hand in the air, giving the signal to the others.

Mac looked back and saw the drone killer had hopped up into its nest. *Damn*. She stood, moving closer. A spray of raptor poison made her curse and dodge back. Something rammed into her, tackling her out of the way. Niko pushed her down and then rolled to his feet. He turned, aimed his carbine and kept fighting.

She'd pay him back later for that bit of alpha-male heroics. But right now, she had to get to the drone killer. Take it down, and then they could escape.

She reached the nest, leaning over it—

Thump. Something hit her in the left shoulder. She jerked, falling to her side. *Thump*. A second hit, in her right shoulder. Pain exploded through her.

She'd been hit. She looked down and saw two bone projectiles sticking out of each shoulder. The kind of projectiles favored by raptor snipers.

"Snipers!" she yelled to the others.

Mac tried to move, the pain making her eyes water. Then she slumped back. The projectiles were pinning her to the nest.

She heard a noise and looked up.
Straight into the green eyes of the drone killer.

Chapter Fourteen

Niko traded punches with a huge raptor.

He knew if the damn thing landed a solid hit, he'd go down and not come back up.

He stepped back and launched into a hard roundhouse kick. It collided with the alien's ugly face and sent it stumbling. He swung his carbine around and took the raptor down.

Niko looked around for Mackenna and spotted her.

His blood ran cold. *No.* She was down and pinned to the nest.

He started pushing through the fighting to get to her. A raptor got in his way and he wasted no time killing it.

When he looked again, he saw the drone killer was striking at Mackenna with its sharp beak. She was rolling her head from side to side to avoid its blows.

Dammit. Another raptor stepped into his path.

It fired its weapon and the poison hit Niko's carbine. He saw it melt and sizzle, and he threw the now-useless weapon aside. He reached in and pulled out his knives.

He spun, jumped up, and slammed the knives

into the raptor's neck, wrenching them back out as the raptor fell to the ground.

Once again, Niko rushed toward Mackenna. He saw the drone killer aiming right at her face. She was yanking on the projectiles, trying to free herself, her face contorted.

He pushed for more speed, but he knew he couldn't reach her in time. He was running, shoving raptors out of his way.

Suddenly, something flew past him and straight in Mackenna's direction, distracting the drone killer.

Lia's drone.

The drone hovered, spun, then raced away. The bird lifted off in pursuit.

Niko covered the last few meters to Mackenna. Beside the ship, he saw the two Hawks materialize. The rest of Squad Nine and Hell Squad were all leaping out onto the deck.

"Hell Squad, ready to go to hell?" Marcus' distinctive voice.

"Hell, yeah," came the chorus of replies. "The devil needs an ass-kicking!"

As the reinforcements joined the fray, the fighting intensified.

Niko reached Mackenna. "Hang on."

Her pained gaze caught his. He gripped the first projectile and pulled. She groaned, long and loud.

"I know. I'm sorry."

"Get the other one out," she rasped.

He gripped it and yanked.

Quickly, he fumbled and pulled his field first aid

kit off his belt. He found some absorbent gauze and pressed it against her shoulder wounds.

Suddenly, she rolled to her side and lifted her carbine. The laser whine was loud in his ears.

He looked back and saw a raptor had been charging up behind them. It crashed down beside them on the deck.

"Thanks."

"Any time," she replied.

A loud squawk pierced the air. The drone and the bird zoomed past overhead.

"We've got to take it down," Mackenna said.

Niko started to nod, but then he heard a sound that made the hairs on the back of his neck stand on end.

A deep, demonic growling.

He'd never seen one in real life, but he knew instantly what the alien doglike creatures were.

Canids.

"Cedar oil grenades," someone shouted.

Niko saw grenades being lobbed at the dogs. "Damn. We have to go, Mackenna. We're out of time." He heaved her up, and seeing the amount of blood she'd lost made his jaw lock. She grimaced.

"Maybe Shaw can shoot the drone killer from the Hawk," Mackenna suggested.

"We can try that. Just focus on getting out of here."

Niko urged her forward, and together, they hobbled towards the nearest Hawk.

He saw Hell Squad was pulling back. All of a sudden, a raptor tossed a grenade. It clanked against the ground and rolled.

"Grenade!" Niko pushed Mackenna down, covering her body with his.

The explosion was deafening. Niko's ears were ringing, all the sound around him muffled.

He realized when he didn't feel any pain that they'd been out of the blast radius. Thank God. He leaped to his feet and pulled her up again.

They ran into Cam and Roth who gave them cover fire.

"On board," Roth said. "It's too hot."

"The drone killer isn't down yet," Niko told him.

"Shit." Roth's face was serious. "Get aboard. We'll find a way to take it down."

Just before they climbed into the Hawk, Lia appeared on deck.

"What are you doing off the Hawk?" Niko demanded.

"My drone, it's hit something near the nest. It's stuck."

Niko's mind raced. Losing another drone wasn't ideal, but the deck of this alien ship was too dangerous. "We'll have to leave it."

Lia shook her head fiercely. "It's close. I can get it. Circle around, give me some cover fire, and come back for me." She ran across the deck.

***

Finn

Finn watched as Hell Squad and Squad Nine

climbed aboard the other Hawk.

Looked like he'd have no passengers for the journey home. Lia had scrambled out with a shout about getting in the other Hawk with her drone.

Then he spotted a small figure running across the deck.

He sucked in a breath. Lia.

What the hell did she think she was doing? He moved his Hawk closer, until he was hovering just off the side of the alien ship. It took him a second, but he spotted the drone hooked up on some sort of tower structure not far from the drone killer nest.

The other Hawk moved toward the back of the ship, laying down laser fire. The raptors were firing back and the canids were loping in that direction.

They were trying to pull the aliens off Lia and her crazy mission to grab the drone.

With his pulse drumming, he saw her reach the drone. She climbed up on a box, but before she could grab it, the drone killer flew out of nowhere and straight into her. She fell the few meters to the ground, landing flat on her belly.

Finn saw the bird start pecking at her, clawing at her armor. She threw her arms over her head, trying to protect herself.

Dammit. He needed to help her. The other Hawk was busy keeping the raptors occupied. In a split second, he made his decision. Finn put his Hawk on auto-hover, grabbed his laser pistol, and leaped onto the deck a few meters below.

He rolled and then ran in Lia's direction. When he reached her, he batted at the drone killer.

"Get off of her!"

With a screech, the bird flew up in the air and toward its nest.

Finn crouched. "Lia? Are you okay?

She lifted her head and nodded. She only had one small trickle of blood at her temple. "Boost me up so I can reach the drone."

He grabbed her around her small waist and lifted her upward. He decided not to point out that his face was practically buried against the curves of her ass.

"I've got it!"

She held the drone out with a smile.

Then Finn spotted the drone killer racing toward them.

"Lia, watch out!" He shot at the bird, saw it veer away.

He heard raptor fire behind them. Finn spun Lia, trying to shield her with his body. Poison splattered across the tower structure in front of them. It caught the hovering drone killer in the chest.

With a God-awful screech, the bird flapped its now-dissolving wings and fell over the side of the ship into the ocean.

Finn ducked, pulling Lia down with him. "This way." He led her around the nest until they had a straight run to his Hawk. "I'll lay down some cover fire, and you run back to the Hawk."

She looked like she was going to argue.

He pressed a finger over her lips. "No. Don't argue, just run." He released her and lifted his laser pistol.

As he fired, he saw her run, arms pumping. He fired at the incoming raptors and saw laser fire from the second Hawk spray across them. Thank God.

He was about to leave, when he heard a noise from the nest. Frowning, he looked inside.

And saw a tiny little drone killer chick.

Fuck. It was tiny and kind of fluffy. Suddenly, it leaped up out of the nest, and into his hands.

Then he heard raptor grunts from nearby, and the clink of a grenade as it rolled across the deck. *Time to go.*

Finn spun and ran towards his Hawk. The grenade exploded behind him, but he just kept running.

Ahead, he saw Lia climbing one of the ropes up into the Hawk. Finn jumped onto the railing and leaped off the side of the ship. He grabbed the rope, swinging wildly, and scrambled up.

Once he was aboard, he slammed the side door closed. He grabbed Lia by the front of her armor, dragging her up on her toes. "*Never* go into a combat zone again."

She lifted her chin. "Screw you, Erickson." Then she reached out, yanked him in close and kissed the hell out of him.

Before he could comprehend what was happening, she pulled back. "Now, get us out of here."

Finn just stared at her dumbly, his body still reeling from that kiss. Her face was completely unreadable, and he had the most painful hard-on he'd had in a long time.

"Finn!" She slapped at his chest. "Get us out of here."

He shook his head to clear it, and climbed into the cockpit. Below, he had a perfect view of where the nest had been sitting. It had been completely destroyed by raptor poison.

He touched the controls and the Hawk shot forward, away from the alien ship. He let out a harsh breath.

Then, Finn felt a movement on his chest. He looked down...and saw the drone killer chick pop its head up out of his pocket.

It chirped at him.

Ah, hell. He shoved it back down into his pocket. He didn't have time to deal with it just yet. Lia climbed into the copilot seat.

"Mention that kiss and I'll deny it," she said.

Finn ignored her and fell in with the other Hawk. Time to head home.

He wasn't going to think of that kiss. Nope. Not once.

He was not going to think about soft lips, a sleek little tongue, and that sweet honeyed taste.

Nope. Never.

Chapter Fifteen

Mac leaned back against Niko as their Hawk traveled back to the Enclave. She hurt like hell.

Taylor was leaning over her, working to stop the bleeding from one of Mac's wounds. Niko held a wad of blood-covered cloth over her other shoulder.

All around them, the Hawk was filled with big, armored bodies. They were covered in spatter and sweat, but they were all jubilant. She saw Shaw fist-bumping with Reed. Sienna knocking her hip against Theron. Marcus and Roth were talking, and both had faint smiles on their faces.

"We did it," Mac murmured.

Niko's lips brushed her ear. "We did. The drone killer is gone."

They'd seen the bird get hit. Watched it slam into the water and disappear.

"You were magnificent," Niko murmured. "Born to fight."

"I think you're biased." Pain speared through her shoulders and made her back arch.

"Maybe." He looked up at Taylor. "Can you give her something for the pain?"

The other woman nodded. "Here you go, Mac."

Taylor put a pressure injector against Mac's neck. "That'll take the edge off."

"I'll owe you a bottle of that wine you like," Mac said. "My man is connected at the Enclave. I'm sure he can snag me a bottle."

"An entire box if you stop her from hurting," Niko promised.

"Your man, huh?" Taylor said with a smile, placing a bandage over Mac's shoulder.

"Yep." Mac tilted her head back, looking into sexy green eyes. "I've decided to keep him. He feeds me, spoils me with daily—"

Niko pressed a hand over her mouth. "She react badly to meds?"

Taylor grinned. "Yep."

He stroked her hair. "Just relax, Mackenna. And maybe don't talk."

She snuggled into him. He was warm, so strong, and so hers. "Okay."

By the time they reached the Enclave, the meds had worn off enough that she wasn't in agony but she could also think straight again. She let Niko help her off the Hawk and when she spotted the other Hawk descending, she breathed a sigh of relief. Finn and Lia had made it.

General Holmes was striding toward them. "Well done. All of you."

"Thank you, sir," Roth said.

The general nodded at Finn and Lia as they reached them. "And you two...thank you. Without your hard work and bravery, the drone killer wouldn't have been eliminated."

"I'm just glad it's gone," Lia murmured.

"Ah, we may have a tiny problem," Finn said.

Mac leaned against Niko, wondering if she'd ever heard such a hesitant tone from the Hawk pilot before.

She watched Finn reach into the top pocket of his flight suit...and pull out a tiny bird.

Everyone in the hangar went quiet.

The tiny, fluffy, black bird chirped at them.

Lia spun to face Finn. "Are you insane? You brought a baby drone killer back with us!"

"I didn't plan it. It jumped in my pocket and I was kind of too busy saving your ass to notice it."

"What if the aliens can track it?" Roth said.

Finn shook his head. "I ran a prelim scan on it in the Hawk. There's no signal coming off of it and it's entirely organic. No alien tech. At least that I can tell."

General Holmes was staring at the small chick. "Well, we'll have to check it out. Maybe we can learn something from it."

Suddenly a body ran into the hangar. Selena's long hair flowed out behind her. "I sensed..." Her green gaze scanned the space. "I sensed my own kind." Then she spied the chick and her entire face lit up, her skin glowing. "A baby gyr."

She moved over to them, holding her hands out. The chick started chirping madly and flapping its small wings. It leaped from Finn's palm and into Selena's.

"The gyr the Gizzida stole must have been pregnant." The alien woman lifted the bird and it nuzzled against her cheek.

Mac smiled. It was the first time she'd really seen Selena look happy and at peace.

"Well," the general said. "I think I know the best person to be in charge of the gyr chick and our study of it."

More people entered the hangar, and Mac saw Doc Emerson in the lead with a team of her technicians pushing hovering iono-stretchers.

Mac stiffened. "I'm not going on a stretcher. I'm walking to the infirmary."

"I don't think so," Niko said.

She pulled a face. "There's your bossy-leader voice again."

Doc Emerson's gaze landed on Mac. "Ahh, Mackenna, looks like you'll be the lucky person getting the needles and nanomeds today."

Mac managed a weak smile. "Lucky me."

***

Mac stood, watching Niko address the crowd in the Garden.

"Thanks to the bravery and skill of Squad Nine, Hell Squad, Devlin Gray, our Hawk pilots, and Lia Murphy of the drone team, the drone killer has been eliminated."

The crowd broke into cheers.

Niko kept talking, telling them about the hope for the future, and how they were now a single group of survivors working together.

He had an easy charm and a steady strength

that people responded to.

And he was all hers.

Her shoulders were still aching from where the projectiles had hit her, although they were all healed up. Niko had stayed by her side the entire time as the doc had patched her up. With him, she felt okay about leaning on someone. She no longer felt the need to be tougher or stronger...she could just be Mackenna.

"Now the hard work begins," Roth murmured from beside her.

She knew what he was talking about. "We have to formulate a plan to take down the Gizzida, once and for all."

Her boss nodded. "We gather our intel, we look for their weak spots, we find a way."

Mac saw his lips turn up into a smile. She followed his gaze and saw that he was staring at Avery, who was over with Santha.

"And we keep living," he said simply.

Mac understood now, and she nodded. She was looking forward to that second bit. She glanced over at Niko. She was looking forward to it a lot.

"So, you and Ivanov?"

Not so long ago, Roth's question would have made Mac nervous. She would've wondered if he was second-guessing her judgment, or considering if she was going soft. Not anymore. "Yes. Me and Niko."

Roth gave a nod. "Good. I like him. Do I need to question him about his intentions?"

Mac snorted. "Only if you want me to kick your ass."

Roth laughed and squeezed the back of her neck. "Roger that."

She looked over to where Niko was now surrounded by people—both Enclave and former Blue Mountain Base. He was patiently answering their questions, smiling, and nodding.

Then she saw a woman with a young girl approaching him. Mac's chest hitched. Anne and her daughter.

Mac had taken a step forward, then stopped. Anne threw herself into Niko's arms, a sad smile on her face. Niko hugged her back, saying something. The woman nodded, and they both drew Anne's daughter into the embrace.

It would soothe that dark hurt in him. Mac smiled. And all of them could start to find a way to heal.

To live.

In her head, Mac started planning something special for her man. "See you later, Roth." She pushed through the crowd and left the Garden.

***

Niko had seen Mackenna sneak off from the talk. After he had finally broken free of the crowd and all their questions, he'd expected to find her in his apartment. But she wasn't there.

He figured she'd turn up, so he'd taken out a piece of wood he'd been saving for the last few months. Now it was speaking to him, and he was carving it in a frenzy.

It was taking shape exactly how he wanted it to.

The door opened. Niko looked over and there she was.

She smiled. "Hi."

"Hi, yourself."

She was carrying a tray and she set it down on the table. Then she moved closer. "What are you working on?"

He just nodded his head toward the wood.

"God, it's beautiful, Niko. You are so talented."

"It's not finished yet."

It was clearly Mackenna. Her slender but strong body pressed back against a man's chest. His hands were covering her breasts possessively, and her face, as she looked up toward him, showed love.

"Is that how I look at you?" she asked quietly.

"It's how I hope you look at me."

She reached out and stroked his hand, following the line of paint staining his skin. "I'm in love with you, Nikolai Ivanov. Who you were, who you are, and who you will be with me."

Niko released a breath, fighting the flood of emotion in him. He pulled her in for a kiss. "God, Mackenna. You bewitched me from the moment you held a gun to my head."

She laughed. "You are so easy. And you're never going to let me live that down, are you?"

"Never. Now that I know you, now that I've held you, touched you, I love you so much." He deepened the kiss, nipping at her lips. Then the two of them were stumbling toward the bed.

She helped him tear his T-shirt over his head, and then she surprised him by pushing him back onto the bed.

"I want to share moments with you, Niko. Sexy, indulgent moments." She grabbed a bottle off the tray she'd brought in. "Vodka?"

He grabbed it from her and took a healthy swig. He enjoyed the burn, but he really didn't need it. Nothing could match the heat she generated in him.

She slowly pulled her clothes off, a sexy little show just for him, until she stood there in pretty black lace panties and matching bra. "I want to spoil you, too." She grinned. "I heard a rumor that you like dark chocolate."

"I do."

She reached out and grabbed a bowl. "I stole some from the kitchen and I melted it." She tipped the bowl up, dripping some of the chocolate onto his chest.

Niko swallowed a gasp. She set the bowl down, climbed up on top of him, and put her mouth on his skin.

Jesus. He reached down and cupped her face. "I love you, Mackenna."

"I love you, too." She lapped at his skin, her gaze never moving from his. "Now how about we make some of those sexy memories together? I seem to recall you promised to spoil me with daily orgasms."

Niko reached down and pulled her against him,

smearing them both in chocolate. He loved the sound of her laugh. "I did, didn't I?" He let his hands skim down her body and got to work.

I hope you enjoyed Niko and Mac's story!

Hell Squad continues with FINN, the story of Hawk pilot, Finn Erickson, and head of the drone team, Lia Murphy. Read on for a preview of the first chapter.

Don't miss out! For updates about new releases, action romance info, free books, and other fun stuff, sign up for my VIP mailing list and get your *free box set* containing three action-packed romances.

Visit here to get started:
www.annahackettbooks.com

FREE BOX SET DOWNLOAD

JOIN THE ACTION-PACKED ADVENTURE!

Formats: Kindle, ePub, PDF

Preview – Hell Squad: Finn

"Finn, get your ass down here!"

Finn Erickson heard Marcus Steele's gravelly voice across the comm line. Finn fired at the alien vehicle on the ground below, and then pulled his Hawk quadcopter into a tight turn. Below, he saw Hell Squad and its leader, Marcus, battling a large raptor patrol. Even though the humans were clad in black carbon fiber armor, they still looked small compared to the giant humanoid aliens.

"I'm coming," Finn said.

"Make it quick," Marcus growled. "Gabe's bleeding like a stuck pig."

Finn touched the controls again, his Hawk responding in an instant. He spotted the big form of Gabe Jackson. The man was fighting with a brutal ruthlessness. He didn't look injured, but Finn expected that as long as he was breathing, a man like Gabe would keep fighting.

Hell Squad had been fighting since the day the aliens had invaded. Finn knew the tough group of soldiers wouldn't stop until the Gizzida were gone.

If they were ever gone.

Finn fired again at another big, ugly, squat alien

vehicle. Then he spotted a good place to land, and started his descent.

He didn't touch the skids to the ground. It was too hot. Instead, he hovered just above the grass. "Make it quick, Marcus."

Ahead, in the distance, he saw more alien vehicles bumping over the now twisted and overgrown patch of road. *Damn, they just keep coming.*

It had been almost two years since the world as they knew it had ended. The Gizzida—dinosaur-like aliens—had arrived out of the blue, in their giant ships. They'd wanted the Earth's resources. The biggest one being humans themselves.

The side door of the Hawk was yanked open. Finn looked back, and saw Hell Squad jumping aboard.

"Finn?" A sweet, feminine voice sounded from his comm panel. "Drone feed is showing incoming pteros."

Elle Milton was the comms officer for Hell Squad, not to mention, Marcus' fiancée.

"I see them, Elle." Finn tapped the screen on his control panel and saw the dots zooming in from the north. He yelled back over his shoulder, "Strap in!"

He sent the Hawk upward at high velocity. He heard a *thump* from the back, and then cursing.

"We have incoming pteros. A lot of them. I need someone on the autocannon."

The alien ships were close enough now that Finn could make out the distinctive pterosaur shape. Large, fixed wings sharpened to a pointed cockpit at the front, along with a long, tail-like back end.

His hands danced over the controls, his Hawk responding instantly. As the raptor ships started firing their deadly poison ammunition, Finn threw the quadcopter into evasive maneuvers.

Flying had been his obsession since he was a boy growing up in Norway. It didn't matter if he was under fire from aliens, or just out for a scenic glide. He loved it.

He heard the autocannon in the back returning fire.

He guessed it was Shaw Baird, Hell Squad's sniper. The guy had a magic touch with any weapon and a hell of an aim.

As they raced across the sky, Finn tried to anticipate the pteros movements, guess where Shaw needed him to be. With some fancy flying, he got Shaw in position twice to take down the alien ships. Finn watched with a satisfied smile as the pteros hit the ground and exploded into balls of flames.

Soon, the remaining pteros turned back, and they were free.

Finn leveled out the quadcopter and turned them toward home base. The Enclave.

The secret human hideaway was built in an old underground coal mine south of Sydney—the former capital of the United Coalition of Countries. The Enclave hadn't been their home for very long. They'd barely been there a month. Their previous base—an old military installation in the Blue Mountains to the west—had been attacked by the aliens. It had sent the Blue Mountain Base survivors on a wild race out of the mountains to find sanctuary. Thankfully, the Enclave had taken them in.

Finn liked the place. It'd been specially designed for the purpose of safely housing people, and was way more luxurious than the retrofitted base in the mountains had been. And, although it had taken a little time, the people of the Enclave were finally warming up to the Blue Mountain Base survivors.

Together, they were stronger. Together, they had a far better chance of driving the Gizzida away.

Finn raised his voice. "Ladies and gentlemen, turbulence has ended. Enjoy the rest of your flight, and thanks for choosing to fly with Erickson Air."

"Can it, Finn."

Finn grinned to himself. The accented voice belonged to Cruz Ramos, Hell Squad's second-in-command.

"Lousy service, though. Where are my drinks and complimentary peanuts?"

That cocky voice belonged to Shaw.

So much had changed in the last two years. Finn had been part of the Coalition Air Force before the invasion, and while he'd flown some combat missions, it had been nothing like what he was doing now. Now, he flew Hell Squad around—the toughest squad that they had. And that was both a privilege and an honor.

Since the invasion, he'd seen too many friends and colleagues die. He had no idea about his family. Pain speared through him briefly, like raptor poison to his chest. His mother, father, and siblings lived in Norway, and to this day, he had no way of knowing what had happened to them. He'd heard Norway had been bombed...but the limited communication they'd had in the early days had been unreliable. And since then, the aliens had found a way to block it.

Finn took a deep breath. He liked to believe that his family was still in their village, way up in the north. Safe.

Soon, the site of the Enclave came into view. From the air, there was nothing to indicate that thousands of survivors were living below the surface. It was all overgrown, rolling hills, the rotted remains of some old coal mines, and the broken ruins of some abandoned towns.

He slowed the Hawk and brought it to a stop, hovering in the air. He reversed the rotors and started lowering. On the control screen, he saw the ground beneath the Hawk open up. The doors of the hangar were opening, creating a gaping hole in the ground.

Soon, the Hawk's skids touched concrete. He powered down the engines, undid his straps, and left the cockpit.

The blood-spattered Hell Squad started to leave the Hawk. He slapped Cruz and Shaw on the back. The men lifted their chins in response.

As Marcus argued with a silent Gabe about heading to the infirmary, Finn watched Shaw toss an arm around Hell Squad's lone female soldier,

Claudia Frost. Somehow, Shaw had convinced the deadly, dark-haired woman to take a chance on him. The two were crazy in love, and the sight of them made Finn grin.

While Hell Squad's job was over, Finn's wasn't. He had to take care of the love of his life. He circled his Hawk slowly, running through the mental checklist of things he needed to inspect.

In the air, she was hidden by a state-of-the-art illusion system that blurred her visually, and made her near-invisible on raptor scans. She ran on a small thermonuclear engine, and with her four rotors shrouded, she was virtually silent.

He moved around to the front of the Hawk, and gave the metal an affectionate pat. "Good job today, baby."

Then he frowned, noting a small patch of what looked like melted metal. Raptor poison must have touched it. He made a mental note to get maintenance to check it out. The damn stuff could burn through anything. Luckily, this looked like a tiny, manageable spot. They only had a limited fleet of Hawks left, and they couldn't afford to lose another. He'd already had the displeasure of crashing one.

He heard footsteps crossing the hangar, in a familiar, crisp, purposeful rhythm. Finn turned his head, and zeroed in on a redheaded woman heading to the office area.

His mouth went dry. Lia Murphy didn't look his way—probably on purpose—so he took his time to study her.

The head of the drone team—the tiny quadcopters they used to gather their intel and spy on the aliens—was of average height, but that's where average ended. She had red hair—not a vibrant wine-red, but a softer red that made Finn think of sunsets. She had a downright beautiful face, and the creamiest skin that Finn had ever seen. She was slender, but there was no missing the full breasts and the gentle curves under her clothes.

She was also annoying, opinionated, and not to mention a hell of a kisser.

For a second, Finn was tossed back to that adrenaline-fueled moment that took place on his Hawk on a previous mission two weeks ago. Hovering over an alien warship, having just taken out the drone killer that had been attacking their drones, Lia had kissed the hell out of him.

"Erickson? Erickson?"

Finn blinked and focused on a stocky, older man in baggy coveralls standing in front of him.

"You want your baby fueled?" the man asked.

"Ahh, sorry. Yes, sure thing, Keith."

The old man shot him a strange look and ambled off, and Finn shook his head, trying to focus. He had work to do. He shouldn't be thinking of luscious redheads, no matter how beautiful they might be. He patted the side of his Hawk again. She was the only woman he needed. She didn't argue with him, she didn't twist him up in knots, and she always did as he asked. That was everything he needed.

***

Lia Murphy sat straight in her chair, listening to the jumble of talking going on around her. It was one of their daily meetings in the Command Center. Marcus from Hell Squad was talking in his deep rasp that made Lia think of gravel and smoke.

"There were more raptor vehicles out on this last mission," the man said. "They're hitting us hard."

General Adam Holmes—the man in charge of security and military operations—nodded. "Our intel is suggesting that. The intel team, with help from the drone team, is slowly increasing our intelligence picture on the aliens. And you're right, we are seeing more alien vehicles on the ground."

"And pteros." This came from Finn Erickson.

Lia didn't look in his direction. The Hawk pilot had confidence down to a fine art. Lia had been a commercial pilot before the invasion, and had met a few combat pilots. Finn fit the mold. Confidence bordering on arrogance.

"So where are they building all these vehicles and pteros?" Cruz asked. "On their mothership?"

The aliens' huge mothership was sitting at Sydney Airport. It was an enormous monstrosity, but Lia couldn't see them manufacturing large vehicles inside of it.

Nikolai Ivanov stepped forward. The dark-haired man was the civilian leader of the Enclave. "We don't know yet. We need to keep looking." The handsome artist looked in Lia's direction. "Lia? Report?"

She cleared her throat and stood. "We have more drones coming online, and we're focused on training more drone pilots."

From behind her, Finn snorted. She ignored him. The man didn't believe flying a drone made you a pilot. *Idiot.*

"The two flight simulators we've set up for training are working out really well. We've asked for volunteers with any sort of flying experience, and we have a good-sized group we're running through the simulations for flying both the drones and the Hawks." She took a breath. "Out in the air, we're slowly covering all the area across Sydney and the regions beyond with the drones. Getting a picture of raptor numbers and their infrastructure." She frowned. "We do have an area where the drone feed is getting jammed frequently. It's happened several times." She looked over at Elle Milton, who was seated behind a comp. "Elle, could you pull up the map for me, please?"

The brunette nodded, and a map appeared on one of the many screens on the wall.

"The area is north of the city, what was originally the Central Coast. Every time we send drones into that area, they get jammed. I suspect the aliens are protecting something."

"What was there before the invasion?" Niko asked.

"It was resort towns, and weekend homes for people who lived in Sydney. Nothing I can think of that would be that interesting to the Gizzida."

Holmes stroked his chin. "Okay, Finn, can you please plan a mission to get up there? We need eyes on the ground to see what's going on." The general's laser-blue gaze circled the room. "I don't need to remind you all how important it is that we fill in all the gaps in our intel grid."

Lia knew it was vital. They needed to have a full picture of the aliens, so they could plan out a strategy to drive the raptors away for good.

"Our other priority," Niko added, "is establishing reliable contact with the other human bases around the world. We already know of the underground base at Groom Lake in Nevada, and a few smaller ones scattered around the globe. But the aliens have been jamming our contact with them for a long time now. We get partial messages that aren't very clear. We don't know their status, if they're still functioning."

Still alive. Lia heard the unspoken words echo in her head.

And following that thought, the familiar sting of grief flowed through her. She knew the people most important to her hadn't made it. It still hurt, even after two years.

"How?" Roth Masters asked. The muscular man was the leader of the almost-all-female squad, Squad Nine. "How can we stop the aliens jamming our long-range communications?"

"The tech team is coming up with a plan," Holmes said. "Noah?"

Noah Kim stepped forward. The tall man always

made Lia think of a pirate, with his long, dark hair combined with an intense, narrow face, and a near-permanent scowl. The man was a genius. "The aliens have blocked our long-range comms because they've managed to destroy the infrastructure between us and the other havens. My team is working to devise what we're calling an amplifier. It's a device that can boost the signal. We are designing it to be watertight, so it can be dropped in the ocean and stay hidden beneath the water. It'll do its job, and hopefully remain invisible to the aliens." He looked around the room. "Anyone want me to go into the technical details?"

"No!"

"Nope."

"No need."

Lia hid her smile. The squads had been subjected to Noah's tech talk in the past, and they weren't fond of it.

Holmes gave a faint smile. "I don't think that's necessary. Thank you, Noah."

Finn was frowning from where he stood, leaning against the wall. "How far out does this thing need to be dropped?"

Noah's face darkened. "At the moment, far. As in, middle-of-the-Pacific far."

Oh, no. Lia straightened. "That's impossible." She knew the Hawks weren't designed to fly that kind of distance. They were made for short-range combat. "We don't have any aircraft that can fly that far."

During the invasion, the Gizzida had very

purposefully destroyed airports and aircraft. There were no supersonic craft left that could make the journey in a fraction of the time. Lia's fingers twitched. She'd flown supersonic jets before the invasion. For a second, she let herself think about that moment when you went supersonic. The slight jerk, the feeling of speed. God, she missed it.

"Once we've finished making the amplifier, I'll let you know." Noah shrugged. "We're still working on the prototype, and I'm hoping we'll be able to devise a way for it to travel itself. That way we can drop it offshore and let it do its thing."

Lia didn't think the man looked particularly hopeful.

"Well, if we keep drowning in pteros, we won't be able to get even one kilometer offshore to drop this thing," Finn said.

The general nodded. "Let's find out where the aliens are manufacturing their vehicles. Make that a priority."

There was a flash of movement, and Lia saw a handsome man in dark trousers and a crisp white shirt step forward. She knew Devlin Gray was a key part of the intelligence team. "Santha and I will make it our team's priority." He glanced at the head of the intel team.

Santha Kade nodded.

"Okay, everyone." Niko shoved his hands in his pockets. Lia noticed a streak of blue paint on his jeans. "Remember, enjoy your downtime. We don't want anyone to get burned out."

The meeting was over. As everyone started to

move out of the Command Center, Sakura—one of Lia's best drone pilots—fell into step beside her.

"Enjoy your downtime. You know why he says that?" the tiny woman asked with a smile.

"Because we're in the middle of a stressful fight for survival? Because it's important to stay sane and find some pleasure where you can?"

Sakura shook her dark head. "The man is snuggled up with Mac from Squad Nine." The woman waggled her eyebrows. "I can only imagine what kinds of things a sexy man like that gets up to in his downtime."

Lia shook her head with a smile. She pictured Mackenna "Mac" Carides. The second-in-command of Squad Nine was a tough, no-nonsense soldier. "I'm not sure Mac snuggles."

Sakura watched Niko stride out of the room. "I bet she does with him."

Lia had to admit, his jeans did great things for his ass. And walking right behind Niko was Finn. He was dressed in black cargo pants, and they did equally good things for the pilot's ass.

She felt a traitorous curl of heat in her belly. Finn might be overconfident and arrogant, but he was good-looking arrogant. He had tousled blond hair, painfully blue eyes, and a body he honed to muscled precision. Hawk flying could be demanding, and Finn made sure he was in peak condition for his job.

Lia blew out a short breath. She wasn't supposed to be thinking about Finn Erickson. She stomped down on her desire. Getting attached to people in this crazy world of theirs made no sense. She'd already had a vital part of her ripped open, broken, and smashed. She would never, ever risk caring for, or loving someone, again.

She looked at her watch. Besides, she had a date to train potential new pilots. That's all she could care about.

Hell Squad

Marcus
Cruz
Gabe
Reed
Roth
Noah
Shaw
Holmes
Niko
Finn

MORE ACTION ROMANCE?

ACTION
ADVENTURE
TREASURE HUNTS
SEXY SCI-FI ROMANCE

When astro-archeologist and museum curator Dr. Lexa Carter discovers a secret map to a lost old Earth treasure—a priceless Fabergé egg—she's excited at the prospect of a treasure hunt to the dangerous desert planet of Zerzura. What she's not so happy about is being saddled with a bodyguard—the museum's mysterious new head of security, Damon Malik.

After many dangerous years as a galactic spy, Damon Malik just wanted a quiet job where no one tried to kill him. Instead of easy work in a museum full of artifacts, he finds himself on a backwater planet babysitting the most infuriating woman he's ever met.

She thinks he's arrogant. He thinks she's a trouble-magnet. But among the desert sands and ruins, adventure led by a young, brash treasure hunter named Dathan Phoenix, takes a deadly turn. As it becomes clear that someone doesn't want them to find the treasure, Lexa and Damon will have to trust each other just to survive.

The Phoenix Adventures

Also by Anna Hackett

Treasure Hunter Security
Undiscovered
Uncharted
Unexplored

Galactic Gladiators
Gladiator
Warrior
Hero

Hell Squad
Marcus
Cruz
Gabe
Reed
Roth
Noah
Shaw
Holmes
Niko
Finn

The Anomaly Series
Time Thief
Mind Raider
Soul Stealer
Salvation
Anomaly Series Box Set

The Phoenix Adventures
Among Galactic Ruins
At Star's End
In the Devil's Nebula
On a Rogue Planet
Beneath a Trojan Moon
Beyond Galaxy's Edge
On a Cyborg Planet
Return to Dark Earth
On a Barbarian World
Lost in Barbarian Space
Through Uncharted Space

Perma Series
Winter Fusion

The WindKeepers Series
Wind Kissed, Fire Bound
Taken by the South Wind
Tempting the West Wind
Defying the North Wind
Claiming the East Wind

Standalone Titles
Savage Dragon
Hunter's Surrender
One Night with the Wolf

Anthologies
A Galactic Holiday
Moonlight (UK only)
Vampire Hunter (UK only)
Awakening the Dragon (UK Only)

For more information visit AnnaHackettBooks.com

About the Author

I'm a USA Today bestselling author and I'm passionate about **action romance**. I love stories that combine the thrill of falling in love with the excitement of action, danger and adventure. I'm a sucker for that moment when the team is walking in slow motion, shoulder-to-shoulder heading off into battle.

I write about people overcoming unbeatable odds and achieving seemingly impossible goals. I like to believe it's possible for all of us to do the same.

My books are mixture of action, adventure and sexy romance and they're recommended for anyone who enjoys fast-paced stories where the boy wins the girl at the end (or sometimes the girl wins the boy!)

For release dates, action romance info, free books, and other fun stuff, sign up for the latest news here:

Website: AnnaHackettBooks.com

Printed in Great Britain
by Amazon